Take the lid off this crate of stories and you will find. . . an iron lion who is worried about rust, a monster who swallows everything he touches, the ghostly Humblepuppy, a toy princess, a fierce giantess and a host of other fascinating and fun characters.

All the stories in the crate have been specially chosen by children's book specialist Pat Thomson. Each and every one is a tried and tested favourite by top children's authors such as Geraldine McCaughrean, Peter Dickinson, Lucy Boston, Joan Aiken and many others.

You won't want to stop reading until you've discovered everything in the crate!

PAT THOMSON is a well-known author and anthologist. She also works with teachers and students – work which involves a constant search for the best short stories, with quality and child-appeal. She is an Honorary Vice-President of the Federation of Children's Book Groups. She is married with two grown-up children and lives in Northamptonshire.

A CRATE

OF STORIES FOR EIGHT YEAR OLDS

COLLECTED BY PAT THOMSON

ILLUSTRATED BY KATE SHEPPARD

CORGI BOOKS

A CRATE OF STORIES FOR 8 YEAR OLDS
A CORGI BOOK: 0 552 529591

First publication in Great Britain

PRINTING HISTORY
Corgi edition published 1997

Set in 13/15pt M.Bembo by
Phoenix Typesetting, Ilkley, West Yorkshire.

Corgi Books are published by Transworld Publishers Ltd,
61–63 Uxbridge Road, Ealing, London W5 5SA,
in Australia by Transworld Publishers (Australia) Pty. Ltd,
15–25 Helles Avenue, Moorebank, NSW 2170,
and in New Zealand by Transworld Publishers (NZ) Ltd,
3 William Pickering Drive, Albany, Auckland.

Made and printed in Great Britain by
Cox & Wyman Ltd, Reading, Berkshire.

Acknowledgements

The editor and publisher are grateful for permission to include the following copyright stories.

Joan Aiken, 'Humblepuppy' from *A Harp of Fishbones* (Cape, 1972), by Joan Aiken, copyright © Joan Aiken Enterprises Ltd. Reprinted by permission of A.M.Heath Limited.

Lucy Boston, 'Linnet's Story' from *The Children of Green Knowe* (Faber and Faber, 1954) by Lucy Boston. Reprinted by permission of Faber and Faber Ltd.

Peter Dickinson, 'The Iron Lion' (Allen & Unwin, 1973). Reprinted by permission of A.P.Watt on behalf of The Hon Peter Dickinson.

Bernard Evslin, 'The Dolphin Rider' from *The Dolphin Rider and Other Greek Myths,* copyright © Bernard Evslin, 1976. Reprinted by permission of Writers House, Inc.

Eva Ibbotson, 'The Brollachan whose Mother was a Fuath' from *The Worm and the Toffee-Nosed Princess* by Eva Ibbotson. Reproduced by permission of Hodder and Stoughton Ltd.

Sheila Lavelle, 'The Queen of Autumn' from *Trouble with the Fiend* (Hamish Hamilton, 1984) by Sheila Lavelle, copyright © Sheila Lavelle, 1984. Reprinted by permission of Penguin Books Ltd.

Geraldine McCaughrean, 'The Princess Mirabelle' copyright © Geraldine McCaughrean 1997. Reprinted by permission of David Higham Associates.

Moira Miller, 'Pearls for the Giantess' from *A Kist of Whistles* (Andre Deutsch, 1990) by Moira Miller. Reprinted by permission of Scholastic Ltd.

Pat Thomson, 'Pale as Death' from *Tales Told After Lights Out* by Pat Thomson. Reprinted by permission of HarperCollins Publishers Ltd.

Martin Waddell, 'The Tough Guys' from *Ip Dip Sky Blue* (Collins, 1990) edited by Mary Hoffman. Reprinted by permission of David Higham Associates.

CONTENTS

A CRATE OF STORIES
FOR EIGHT YEAR OLDS

The Queen of Autumn

If there's one thing Angela can't stand it's me being better than her at anything. And spoiling my lovely party dress was one of the nastiest things she ever did.

I had made the dress for the Autumn Fête, which we have at school every year in October to raise money for sports equipment and stuff. The funny thing is, we never seem to get any new sports equipment, and I bet you anything you like the parents and teachers spend all the money on the wine and cheese party they have afterwards.

Anyway, the best part of the day is the children's fancy dress competition, and you should just see the brilliant prizes they give. Every year they choose a different theme, nursery rhyme characters or TV advertising or something like that, and the rule is that all the costumes have to be home-made. The theme this year was 'Autumn' and I racked my brains for ages without any success. There was only a week left when at last I had an idea.

My mum keeps all her scraps of fabric that she has left from dressmaking and curtains and stuff, and I was rummaging around in the box among the silks and cottons and velvets when I came across a big piece of the most autumny-looking material you ever saw. It was soft and shiny, with a swirly pattern of misty shapes in red and orange and gold and brown. I stared at it for a minute, then I folded it over my arm and went to find my mum.

'Yes, it's nice, isn't it?' she said, chopping apples at the kitchen table. 'I bought it in a remnant sale years ago. Pity I never got round to doing anything with it.'

'Can I have it, please, Mum?' I said, sliding my arm round her waist and putting on a pleading look like Daniel does when you're eating sausages. 'It'll make a lovely costume for the fancy dress party. The Queen of Autumn, I'm going to be.'

'What a nice idea,' said my mum. 'The colours are perfect. Of course you can have it. But I don't want to find my sewing-box in a mess. Put everything back when you've finished.' I gave my mum a smacking great kiss on the cheek.

'Thanks, Mum,' I said. 'You're my best friend.'

2

'I thought Angela was,' said my mum with a smile.

'She's not any more,' I said, scowling. 'I'm sick of her and her rotten jokes. I'm not playing with her ever again.'

'You've said that hundreds of times,' grinned my mum, and went back to her apples.

I was still mad at Angela over that chocolate cake. It really was a horrible trick. I had called round to see her the evening before, and had found her in the kitchen, sticking chocolate drops into the icing of a big scrumptious-looking chocolate gateau. Chocolate cake is my favourite kind, especially with chocolate butter cream and chocolate icing and chocolate buttons on top.

'Wow,' I said. 'What a fabulous cake.'

Angela put her head on one side as she placed the last chocolate drop in the icing. Then she slid the cake towards me across the table.

'Have a slice, if you like,' she said.

I gazed at the cake doubtfully. 'No, I'd better not,' I said. 'Your mum might not want it cut into yet.'

'Don't be silly,' said Angela, sitting on the lid of the chest freezer and swinging her legs. 'She won't mind. She makes them all the time, you know she does. She likes people to eat them. Go on, Charlie, have a bit. I can see you're dying to.'

I suppose my greed must have got the better of my doubts because I got a knife and cut myself a big wedge. Angela watched me tucking in and there was such a sly expression on her face that I began to feel very uncomfortable.

'Aren't you having any?' I asked, my mouth full of butter-cream filling.

'No fear,' she said. 'My mum will go up the wall. She made that cake specially for the fête on Saturday. You won't half catch it when she sees it now.'

My eyes bulged out of my head and I choked half to death. The cake suddenly tasted like something off the compost heap and I pushed the half-eaten slice hastily away from me. I was wiping my chocolatey fingers on my hanky when Auntie Sally came in. She gave a little shriek of horror when she saw the cake.

'Angela!' she said. 'I told you not to eat any of that cake. I told you it was for the fête. You never listen to a thing I say.'

Angela put on a hurt expression. 'It wasn't me,' she declared virtuously. 'I never touched it, honest. Did I, Charlie?'

My throat went dry and my face went red. I felt like opening the freezer and shoving her in and holding her down until her bottom froze.

'It was me, Auntie Sally,' I gulped. 'I'm sorry. I didn't know it was for the fête.'

Auntie Sally looked at Angela and then at me. She must have seen how upset I was.

'Angela should have told you,' she sighed at last. 'Never mind, Charlie. I can always make another one. And you might as well finish that piece, now you've started it.'

But somehow I wasn't hungry any more. I turned and ran for the door and I was almost home when Angela caught up with me.

'Wait, Charlie,' she called. 'It was only a joke.'

'Some joke,' I shouted, glaring at her. 'You can just keep your jokes to yourself in future, because I'm not playing with you any more.'

'Please yourself,' shrugged Angela. 'See if I care.' And she flounced off home with her nose in the air.

Well, you can imagine how surprised I was when I was in my room cutting up that nice material for my costume and I heard Angela's voice downstairs. I quickly bundled the cloth into a drawer and picked up a book, pretending to read. After a few minutes Angela appeared in the doorway, looking sheepish and holding out one of her most cherished possessions. The lovely peacock's tail feather that she got when she went to Dorset for her holidays.

'I don't want to talk to you,' I said grumpily.

'Please, Charlie. I've brought you my best feather,' she said humbly. 'To say I'm sorry and can we be friends.' She gazed at me with those big blue eyes. 'I'm not going to be horrible to you any more, Charlie. Honest.'

'I don't believe you,' I said. 'Just get lost, will you?'

Angela took a couple of steps into the room. 'I mean it, Charlie,' she said earnestly. 'I know I've been rotten to you sometimes. But a person can change, can't they?' And she looked so sorry for herself I hadn't the heart to be cross any more.

'All right then,' I said, a bit grudgingly. 'But the very next time you do a thing like that . . .' I took the feather and put it in a jar on the window sill where the sunshine could light up the colours.

Angela took a flying leap onto my bed and trampolined in delight. Just when I was expecting my mum to start shouting about all the thumping and banging, she flopped down flat on her back and lay staring at the ceiling.

'What are you wearing for the fancy dress party?' she asked casually. I eyed her suspiciously. Now I knew why she was so keen to make friends.

'I haven't made my mind up yet,' I fibbed quickly, crossing my fingers behind my back. I certainly had no intention of telling her my idea. She was quite capable of pinching it herself.

'It's ever such a hard subject,' complained Angela, screwing up her face. 'I've thought and thought and I still can't think of a thing. What does autumn make you think of, Charlie?'

I looked out of the window into the back garden where my dad was filling another basket with apples from our tree. Daniel was happily chewing one to bits on the lawn.

'Apples,' I said. 'You could go as an apple.'

Angela sat bolt upright and stared at me.

'What do you mean, I could go as an apple? How could you make an apple costume? Don't be so bloomin' stupid.'

'It would be easy,' I said, thinking hard. 'You could cut two great big enormous apple shapes out of cardboard. You could join them together with little straps at the shoulders and sides. You know, like a sandwich-board man. You could paint the card all lovely red and green apple colours. You could even make a hat out of a tube of paper and paint it to look like a stalk.'

Angela's eyes widened. 'And I could have green paper leaves, growing out of the stalk,' she said, getting excited. 'It would be great. Charlie, you're a genius.'

She leapt off the bed and started dancing about. Then she came over and gave me a hug.

'But what about you, Charlie?' she said. 'What about your costume?'

'Oh, don't worry. I'll think of something,' I said. The less she knew about that, the better.

Well, of course I had to help her with the costume, because she's pretty useless at that sort of thing. So we went down into the garden to find my dad and ask him for some cardboard.

He found us a huge flat box that the new wardrobe kit had been delivered in, and he cut out the two big apple shapes for us with his Stanley knife. We carried them upstairs to my room and spread some newspapers out on the carpet to stop my mum from having hysterics. Then we got busy with the nice thick poster paints that my Uncle Barrie sent me last Christmas.

We made the apple rosy red on one side and a sort of yellowy green on the other and it really did look great. When the paint was dry we stapled some strips of card to the tops and sides of the shapes and Angela tried the costume on. And I couldn't help rolling about laughing when I saw her, with only her head and her feet sticking out.

'Come on, Charlie,' she said, grinning at me. 'Let's go and show your dad.'

She had to go sideways through the door and down the stairs and she kept bumping into things and saying 'Ooops'. We were helpless with the giggles by the time we reached the garage, and my dad made us even worse.

'I can see you're going to live appley ever after,' he told Angela. And she lurched crazily round the garage, making Daniel bark his head off.

So off she went home, as pleased as anything with her costume, and she took my big pot of strong glue with her so she could have a go at making a stalk hat and some leaves.

'I'll bring it back when I've finished with it,' she promised.

9

I hardly saw Angela at all that week. Every evening after school I went straight home and worked on my costume, and I didn't half enjoy myself, all cosy and peaceful in my room with the radio on and Daniel snoozing on a rug beside the radiator.

I'm not much good at sewing, so all I did with my mum's material was make a simple tunic by folding it in half and making a hole in the middle for my head. The tunic came right down to my feet and I fastened it round the waist with a gold dressing-gown cord my dad lent me. There was a spare bit of material left to make a short matching cloak, and I sewed on some bits of gold velvet ribbon for the ties at the front.

And now came the nicest part of all. I borrowed my mum's big shopping basket and went out into the country lanes round the edge of the village and I started to collect all the autumn fruits and berries and nuts and dried flowers I could find. There were rose hips and hawthorn berries and conkers and hazelnuts and acorns. There were long trailing strands of some sort of creeper with fluffy white seed heads. There were ears of corn and barley and all sorts of other stuff I didn't know the names of. I brought them all home and set to work with a sharp needle and some strong thread and I made a great pile of the most beautiful jewellery you ever saw.

I made garlands to hang round my neck like the Hawaiian girls do, only mine were made out of dried flowers and grasses. I strung together long necklaces of rose hips and hawthorn berries, and did the same with the acorns and conkers after my dad had drilled holes in them for me with his Black and Decker. I made bangles and bracelets and girdles and even things to go round my ankles. And you should have seen how all those lovely reds and browns and golds and yellows glowed together like precious stones.

Last of all I made a golden crown. I cut it out of card and covered it with gold foil and decorated it with flowers and nuts and berries and ears of wheat. Angela still hadn't brought back my pot of glue, but my dad lent me a tube of superglue which worked even better.

Every day at school Angela would say, 'Have you finished your costume yet, Charlie?' and every day I shook my head. She was dying to know what it was, but I wouldn't tell her a thing. She could find out on Saturday, when it would be too late for her to pinch my idea.

I finished the costume on Friday evening. I put the final touches to the crown and dressed myself up in the whole outfit. I was grinning at my reflection in the mirror when my dad popped his head round the edge of my door.

'Wow,' he said. 'You don't half look smashing. Hey, Liz!' he bellowed down the stairs. 'Come and get an eyeful of our Charlie. She's a right bobby-dazzler.'

I looked in the mirror and I knew he was right. I don't quite know what it was, but I had never looked so nice in my whole life. Something about my dark hair and suntanned face and brown eyes seemed to set off the autumn colours of my costume and make them glow even brighter. I couldn't wait for Saturday to come and I was sure I would win a prize.

Saturday morning was chaotic with everybody dashing about all over the place. My mum's kitchen was so full of sliced bread you could hardly move. Auntie Sally came round to help bake the scones and the fairy cakes, and she brought with her another chocolate gateau like the one I'd cut a chunk out of.

And do you know, she never said one word about the first one. She only gave me a wink and a quick smile and I could have hugged her. I sometimes can't help wishing that Angela was as nice as her mother.

I did my best to help with the sandwiches and things, but I kept on being told to get out of the way. So in the end I went outside into the garden to help my dad instead.

It was one of those beautiful autumn days when the air is warm and still and the light is sort of golden and everything in the garden looks pleased with itself. My dad was sweeping up the fallen leaves and putting them in a big pile at the end of the garden, and Daniel was bouncing about chasing the broom and barking and diving into the heap of leaves looking for imaginary rabbits. I got a rake out of the shed and gave them a hand for a while, and it was much nicer than being in that hot steamy kitchen.

My dad went off and got us all some fish and chips for lunch and we ate them in the garden straight out of the paper to save the washing-up, which I think is the very nicest way to eat fish and chips. Angela and her dad came back from delivering cakes to the tea tent and joined us in the garden and it was like a party.

At last it was time to get dressed for the fête. We decided it was better for Angela and me to walk to school so we wouldn't spoil our costumes, so my mum and Auntie Sally and Uncle Jim went off in the yellow Mini, leaving my dad to follow later with us kids. Angela ran next door to get into her costume, and I hurried upstairs to get myself ready.

I was just settling my crown more firmly on my head when I heard this funny scraping and thumping noise on the stairs and Angela appeared, easing herself sideways round the door. I started to giggle as soon as I saw her.

She had green tights on and green shoes and she had completed the apple costume with a green stalk hat. A big bunch of green paper leaves dangled from the stalk around her face, which she had also painted green. She was carrying my big pot of glue in her hand.

'You look great,' I said admiringly, turning from the mirror to look at her properly.

'Thanks, Charlie,' she grinned, 'I've brought your glue back. Where shall I put it?' And then she gave a long whistle through her teeth as she suddenly noticed my costume.

She stared at me for a long time without saying a word and her eyes went all glittery and strange. She came a bit closer and stared harder and I felt like laughing even more because somebody in a cardboard apple outfit with their face painted green looks ever so funny when they get mad.

And Angela was mad, I could tell. She was so mad she was almost spitting.

of leaves and howled my head off.

My dad found me there a couple of minutes later.

'There, there, bonny lass,' he said, kneeling besides me and patting my shoulder helplessly. 'What's brought all this on?'

I sat up and flung my arms around his neck and blurted out the whole story, but it was so muffled by the sobs and the hiccups and the leaves that at first he didn't seem to understand.

'Glue? What glue?' he said. 'Angela what? She spilt it on your dress?' He gave me his big hanky and I mopped my face. I blew my nose hard and told him all over again what had happened.

'Maybe she didn't do it on purpose,' he said, not sounding very convinced. He helped me to my feet and then stepped back to look at me. I didn't half feel stupid standing there covered in leaves from head to foot.

'Charlie,' said my dad, smiling broadly all over his face. 'Your friend has done you a good turn. She hasn't spoilt your costume at all. She's made it even better.'

I looked down at my dress and my tears suddenly vanished like magic when I saw what he meant. Hundreds and hundreds of autumn leaves had stuck to the glue and the front of my skirt was covered in them. They looked just perfect, all shades of gold and red and orange and brown, and the best thing was that they were real leaves. Much nicer than any old dress material.

My dad picked up my crown from where it had rolled away into the flower-bed and put it back on my head.

'Hang on, pet,' he said. 'I'll get the rest of the glue.' In no time at all he was back with the jar of glue in his hand and he helped me to stick more leaves to the sides and the back of my skirt until I was covered in them from my waist to my feet.

'That'll show them,' he said, looking at me with his head on one side. 'You're the bonniest Queen of Autumn I've ever seen. Now let's get a move on. The judging starts in ten minutes.'

So we dragged Daniel away from his bone and got his lead on him and hurried along to the school field with me rustling like mad and shedding leaves at every step. And I was just in time to join the end of the procession as they paraded around the edge of the judge's arena.

There were clowns and pirates and cowboys and Indians and hardly anybody had taken any notice of the autumn theme. As soon as I got near the judge's table I knew they liked me because they made me stop and turn round in front of them and

Miss Collingwood asked me all sorts of questions about how I had made the costume and whether the leaves had been my own idea.

'A friend helped me,' I said, and they nodded and smiled and said how ingenious it was. Then at last the headmistress went to the microphone to announce the winners.

'Perhaps "Autumn" was rather a difficult theme,' she began. 'But I'm very pleased to see that one or two people have made a real effort to meet the challenge. Third prize goes to Mark Adamson, as a haystack.'

19

Everybody clapped and cheered as little Mark Adamson from Form One, baled up in straw from head to foot, walked out to collect his prize.

'Second prize,' Miss Collingwood went on, 'goes to Angela Mitchell, Form Five, for her extremely clever apple costume.' The crowd whistled and stamped and you should have seen the way that Angela Mitchell danced about and showed off.

Then we all held our breath as Miss Collingwood looked at the bit of paper in her hand. Everybody went quiet, waiting to hear the name of the winner.

'The judges are all agreed on the winner,' said Miss Collingwood, smiling. 'And we have no hesitation in awarding First Prize to Charlotte Ellis, for her delightful Queen of Autumn. We particularly liked the way she used the natural fruits and flowers and leaves of the season to decorate her costume.'

The crowd all clapped like mad and I felt myself go all pink with pride and delight, right there in front of all those people. I could see my dad going even pinker and my mum looking dead pleased and smug.

And then I looked at Angela, and I found a huge grin spreading over my face because she was tearing off her apple costume and ripping it to shreds and jumping up and down on it.

The prize turned out to be four tickets for a London pantomime, with fifty pounds cash to spend on a slap-up meal afterwards.

'We'll take Angela, shall we?' said my mum, as we strolled happily home with Daniel later that afternoon. 'To use up the spare ticket?'

'Not likely,' said my dad. 'I wouldn't take her if she was the last person on earth.'

'I'd rather take a rattlesnake,' I said, and my dad gave a snort of laughter.

In the end we took the new girl, Nicola Daley, and we all had the time of our lives. Angela went wild when she heard about it. But I didn't care. She only got what she deserved, after all.

This story is by Sheila Lavelle.

The Princess Mirabelle

It was a mistake. Father Christmas is usually so careful! But just that once, he simply made a mistake. He gave Kagon SuperLord to Melanie, and to Tyrone he gave the toy princess. Yes, Tyrone got Princess Mirabelle, with her two ball gowns and six pairs of shoes and all those pretty clips for her hair.

Melanie cried.

Tyrone had not cried since he was three, but tears of rage squeezed between his lids as he crushed the plastic packaging. Princess Mirabelle knew at once, by the tightening grip round her waist, that she was not wanted.

First he threw her across the room. Then his brothers Kev and Lennox ran in and asked, 'What did you get? What did you get?' And just in the nick of time, Tyrone managed to kick the Princess out of sight under a pile of clothes.

Somehow he got his brothers out of the bedroom and away downstairs. Mirabelle peeped out in terror. 'What terrible place is this?' she asked.

Bomber planes hung from the ceiling, slime monsters lurked under the bed. A tank pointed its gun directly at her. A robot lay on its side glaring at her with orange eyes.

Mirabelle twirled into the open. Where were her shoes? Where was her other pretty dress? Where was someone to brush her hair and cry out in wonder at her loveliness? Her mother the Queen had always told her: 'One day your Girl will come, and she will gaze and comb and hug and treasure you, as a Princess should be treasured.'

A rubber tarantula bulged out of Tyrone's half-empty Christmas stocking. Trying not to look at it, Mirabelle tiptoed towards the bin where her second dress of gossamer tulle and diamonds glistened like angel wings. But the sound of feet on the stairs sent her diving back among the clothes.

It was Tyrone. He snatched her up, glaring at her so ferociously she thought she would die of fright. He held her up by her hair; he held her up by her feet. 'I'll have to turn it into something else,' he said.

So he wrapped her in foil and pretended she was a robot. But Mirabelle did not stand up without her shoes, and the foil would not stay put.

He cut off her hair, *snip, snip, snip,* and put her in a sock with holes. But she still did not look like Kagon SuperLord; she looked like a doll in a sock.

He tied her to a leg of the bed and got out his cowboy fort. Small, savage braves danced whooping round her, but Princess Mirabelle only straightened her back and raised her short-cropped head, and did not blink an eye, would not give them the satisfaction of seeing she was afraid.

At last the cavalry arrived to rescue her, and Tyrone began a new game. He rammed her legs into a truck and crashed it against the wall. Sequins fell like teardrops from Mirabelle's golden sheath dress, but Mirabelle shed not a tear. 'Some day my Girl will come,' she said, 'and all this will fade like a bad dream.'

After lunch, Tyrone tied a handkerchief to her with four pieces of thread. He wrapped the handkerchief round and round, then opened the window wide.

Reeling and spinning beneath were all the gardens of Sugby. Tyrone lived high, high up – at the top of Jack's beanstalk, Mirabelle supposed. And there, below, like symbols on a map, lay houses, a playground, a park, a busy road with traffic rushing by.

Once, twice, three times, Tyrone whirled her round and then – 'Tyrone! The cartoons are on!' – she was lain down on the window sill, while starlings went wheeling by.

Princess Mirabelle tried to creep back inside. But there, glaring up at her from the floor, were *The Enemy*.

'Go,' said the robot, flashing its orange eyes. 'Can't you see you're not wanted here?'

'Go!' said the slime monsters. 'Can't you see you've upset him?'

'Go!' said the tarantula. 'You should never have come here. You're just a mistake.'

'GO!' they all said, '*PRINCESS!*' And they made it sound like the most ugly word in the language.

Mirabelle rolled sideways off the sill. She fell like a stone, wondering, amid her fear, *Where was my Girl?*

Then suddenly, the handkerchief-parachute opened, and she drifted down, down, this way and that. Just when Mirabelle thought she might live out the day, she realized she was heading for the road!

By pulling the right threads, she managed to steer her descent towards the telephone cables. With a sickening lurch, the parachute tangled, and Mirabelle was left swinging in space.

Cutting herself free, she climbed, hand-over-hand along the wire to where the branches of a tree reached out below her. And then she jumped!

The branch took her weight, and she clambered down, through boughs and birds' nests, to the roof of a garden shed. Such luck that she had no long hair to tangle in the twigs!

Miaow! – a cat pounced. But it was easy to slide down the shed roof, wriggle along the gutter and worm down the drainpipe to the garden path. Old cobwebs slowed her fall.

There was a car parked in the drive. She would run across the lawn, keeping low, and hide in the exhaust pipe until she could spy out the lie of the land. Fortunately her gold dress was hidden by Tyrone's moth-eaten sock; no-one would see a flicker of gold in the long grass.

But half-way across the lawn, she came across the saddest sight she had ever seen. A prince of incomparably good looks lay, wrapped in a satin headscarf, in a shoebox. He had no sword or laser-gun by his side. He had no armour. Only a pink satin hair ribbon had been bound round his legs like a bandage. Mirabelle thought at first he was dead. But when she kissed him, he stirred, opened his eyes and sat up.

'I am Princess Mirabelle,' she said. 'Here, you must wear my sock.'

'I am Kagon SuperLord,' he said. 'Here. Wrap this scarf around you.'

'I was a mistake,' she said.

'So was I,' he said. 'Father Christmas should have left me next door, with my Boy.'

'Then this is the home of . . . my Girl. Did she do this to you? Well I never. So near and yet . . .'

They sat for a moment. It began to rain, and the Christmas raindrops washed the mud and cobwebs off Mirabelle's sheath dress of gold lamé.

'They don't deserve us,' Kagon said.

'I don't believe they do, my dear,' said Princess Mirabelle.

And so they crept stealthily away into the rhodo-dendrons, and bivouacked there before setting off for the uplands of the rockery and the Great World Beyond.

This story is by Geraldine McCaughrean.

The Iron Lion

Let us start with Yasmin, Princess of Persia. She rose, pale and angry, from her jewelled footstool beside the Emperor's throne. Her voice was cool and you could hear it all across the crowded courtyard.

She said, 'Since the Prince of Gascony is so courteous as to ask, I will tell him that I propose to marry the prince who brings to the court of Persia, dead or alive, the Iron Lion of Ferdustan.'

At the name of that dread beast all the ladies in the court fainted, and a number of the nobles only stayed upright by clutching the agate pillars. The Prince of Sybaris giggled, and the Prince of Athens said something in Chinese. But the Prince of Gascony stamped his mailed heel on the pavement, shouted 'Fiddlesticks!' and strode clanking out.

Now let us go back to the beginning.

'Handsome *and* brave *and* kind *and* clever!' cried the Emperor. 'Impossible!'

'Please, Father,' said Yasmin.

'I suppose we can try. But I promise you, my darling, that you couldn't have asked for anything more impossible, not even if you'd said you'd marry the prince who brought you the Iron Lion of Ferdustan.'

So word went out that the Princess of Persia's hand was available to a suitable applicant, and the princes came flocking. For not only was Yasmin very beautiful, but also she was her father's only child. The prince who married her would one day be master of an empire that stretched from ruined Carthage to the tinkling temples below Mount Everest.

There were dances and feasts every evening, and hunting and games every day, and quiet walks between whiles, so that the princes could show off their gifts and graces. And some turned out to be two of the things Yasmin wanted, and some even three, but not a prince in all the world was hand-some *and* brave *and* kind *and* clever.

So the day came when the last three princes in all the world* stood in the agate courtyard to hear

* Except one.

30

the Princess's choice. And to show you what sort of princes they were I'll tell you why they were so late and what sort of gifts they had brought. The Prince of Sybaris had found a strain of oysters that tasted of honey, and he had been waiting to see if they bred true. He had brought a shipload of his oysters. He was kind and clever, but neither handsome nor brave. The Prince of Athens had been learning Chinese in order to impress Yasmin with Chinese odes. He had brought a little old black book which he said was the most precious thing in the world because it was written in a language no-one could read. He was clever, certainly, and might have been handsome if he'd washed and stood up straight, but he'd never given himself the chance to be either kind or brave. And the Prince of Gascony had been besieging a town. He had brought twenty thousand spears. He was handsome and brave, but not very clever and not at all kind.

The trumpets blew and the gongs groaned and the Emperor stood up to speak to the thronged court.

'Your Highnesses, and all my people, I need not say how flattered we are that three such mighty princes have come to seek the hand of our unworthy, hideous and impoverished daughter.

And there lies our difficulty. For if we were to choose one of these lords, we must certainly offend the other two — a course which the ruler of our ridiculous and feeble empire does not dare to take. Therefore, the only answer is that we must decline all three, which now, with tears and lamentations, I do.'

It was a polite way of saying 'No'. But it did not work. For the Prince of Gascony stamped his mailed heel on the floor, so that the sparks flew, and cried, 'We are the last three princes in all the world.★ If the Princess is too proud to marry one of us, whom will she marry? Some woodcutter's son?'

That was when Yasmin rose from the jewelled footstool and said what she said, and when the ladies fainted and the nobles reeled, and when the Prince of Gascony said what *he* said and strode out. Then the Prince of Athens went home and forgot his grief in writing a book against women, and the Prince of Sybaris went home and consoled himself by inventing gravy. But the Prince of Gascony went home and told his army to sharpen their spears. They were a small army, but good.

The other princes put on their armour and girt on their swords and galloped across the Last Desert

★   Except one, but he didn't know that.

to the Red Hills, where no rain ever falls and where the Iron Lion lived. He gobbled them up. Their armour added iron to his diet, so his coat grew stronger and glossier than ever.

Of course, not all the princes of the world got gobbled up, or there would be no Royal Families today. Some lost their way, and some had second thoughts, and besides there was one prince whom everybody had forgotten about. He was working in a circus. His name was Mustapha and he was the Prince of Goat Mountain.

Mustapha's father had been a king who had written a book about the Art of War and had then gathered an army and fought all his neighbours to see if his book was right. When the battles were over, all he had left of his kingdom was Goat Mountain, which none of his neighbours wanted. He had died of boredom, which was how Mustapha found himself ruling an ugly lump of rock and thorn trees on which lived eleven goatherds and their families and thirty thousand goats. After a while, Mustapha saw that he too might die of boredom, so he called the goatherds to his tent. George, the head goat, came also.

'My friends,' said Mustapha, 'I am going out into the world to seek a new kingdom.'

The goatherds threw up their hands.

'Ai-eeeeeeeee,'* they cried. 'Who will rule us? What will become of us?'

'I have thought of that,' said Mustapha. 'You will rule yourselves. Once a week you and George will meet in this tent. If anything needs to be done, and all twelve of you agree, then you will do it. If you do not agree, you will do nothing.'

'Oy-ooooooool,'** cried the goatherds. 'This is a new thing!'

'We will start now,' said Mustapha. 'I need to go into the world to seek a new kingdom. Do you agree?'

'Of course, of course,' said the goatherds, for who were they to deny their Prince his wishes, however mad? George nodded his head.

So Mustapha left Goat Mountain to seek a new kingdom. Unfortunately, he had never been taught anything except the princely arts, so he found it difficult to make enough money to buy bread. When he tried to be a carpenter he hit his thumb with the hammer. When he tried to be a waiter in a restaurant he fell in the soup. Walking unhappily through Baghdad, wondering whether to go back to Goat Mountain, he came to a sign saying,

* This is what goatherds say when they are dismayed.
** This is what goatherds say when they are astonished.

34

Now, among the princely arts is the management of horses, so Mustapha went in and asked for the owner. He was shown a short fat man with a droopy moustache sitting on a barrel eating noodles.

'Vat you vant?' said the fat man.

'I wondered if I could have a job helping with the horses.'

'Ve only a liddle circus are,' grumbled Herman.

'But it says you're the biggest circus in the world.'

'Dese sign writers, dey leave der vord out. Ve der biggest *liddle* circus in der vurld are. If you vant a job vit der horses, you a clown must be also. Are you a clown?'

'In my last job I fell in the soup.'

Herman smiled suddenly, beautifully, like sunrise.

'Ach, you a *great* clown vill be! Have some noodles.'

That was how Mustapha came to join a circus. He liked working with the animals. The lion tamer became a special friend, and taught him some of his art. But the important thing was that Herman was right – Mustapha became a great clown. He did his tricks on a stolid, huge mare called Dapple. The clowns would be in the ring throwing custard pies at each other, and Mustapha would trundle in on Dapple, and the clowns would gang up on him. Just as they all threw their pies Dapple would give a great kick and Mustapha would soar into the air and the pies would pass beneath him and hit all the other clowns in the face. Then they'd chase him around the ring, while the audience roared and stamped and hiccuped. He was dangling upside down under Dapple's belly with his face covered with custard pie when he first saw Yasmin. She was in the Royal Box, laughing. He said, 'That is the girl I'm going to marry.'

(She had been bored at court, now that there were few feasts and no dances, no hunts, no games, so she'd come to the circus to cheer herself up.)

After the circus was over Mustapha went out into the streets to ask about the girl he'd seen, and a man in a purple hat told him the story of Yasmin. Next day the hot weather was beginning, and the circus would close down, so he went to Herman to ask for his wages.

'Ach, dis is foolishness!' cried Herman. 'You a great clown are, and you vant to change dat to be a prince. Dis lion vill gobble you up.'

'Perhaps,' said Mustapha. 'But maybe I am the only prince in the world who knows anything about lion taming. So may I take my wages please?'

Herman shook his head.

'Ach, mein friend, it a terrible season has been. You take Dapple. Ven der cool vedder comes and you dis Iron Lion nonsense have forgotten, you bring her back, I buy her from you, and dat vill be your vages.'

'All right,' said Mustapha, and rode home, earning his keep on the way by clowning in the villages. At Goat Mountain the Council had met once a week in his absence, but had never needed to do anything. Now he told them his plans.

'Ai–eeeeeeeee,' they cried. 'The Iron Lion will gobble you up!'

'Perhaps,' said Mustapha, 'but I want to go. Have I your permission?'

At that moment George scrambled to his feet and dashed out of the tent.

'Come back!' cried Mustapha. 'We cannot decide anything without you.'

'Come back!' shouted the goatherds.

They all streamed out of the tent. It was early night. A big moon was rising and in its slanting light George's eyes gleamed like a demon's a few yards ahead. They ran towards him, and he skipped off. Whenever they ran, he ran, and whenever they stopped to puff and pant George stopped and stared back, green-eyed. In this way he led them around the back of the mountain, along goat paths, to a place where none of them had ever been before. There he waited by a black pool and let himself be caught. Fat Hassan came wheezing up last of all and stooped to the pool for a drink. At once he spat the stuff out and cried 'Oy-ooooooool!' Mustapha and

the other goatherds dipped their fingers into the pool and tasted. It was disgusting, but unlike any taste they had ever tasted before. Mustapha stood and considered.

'It seems to me,' he said, 'that George brought us here because he thinks that this stuff will be useful to me in my adventure with the Iron Lion.'

The long, hairy head nodded.

'I will take two goatskins of this stuff with me.' said Mustapha.

'You can't,' grumbled Hassan. 'If it hasn't got a name, it isn't anything, so you cannot take it.'

'Then we will give it the name you first called it. Oy-ooooooool.'

The goatherds tried the word around their tongues.

'Oy-ooooooool. Oyoool. Oyool. Its name is Oil!' they shouted.

'Good,' said Mustapha, now owner of the first oil well in the world.

Next morning, with his Council's permission, he set off on his journey. In one saddlebag he carried his clown costume, to earn his lodging in the villages on the way. In the other he carried his father's armour. He spent the evenings cleaning and mending the armour, but just when he had got it all gleaming and princely he had to spend a dewy night in the open, and the whole suit rusted again — except, Mustapha was surprised to notice, in one place where the oil had leaked a little from a goatskin. When he wiped it off, that patch glistened as bright as new.

It was a long journey. He fought no dragons, rescued no maidens, but he left a lot of villages more cheerful than they'd been before he came. And at last he rested one night, tired with clowning, in a village on the very edge of the Last

Desert. A fire glowed in the centre of the village square, and the elders sat round it and nodded their beards and talked of the Iron Lion.

'Ah, he's a great beast,' said one.

'Big as a barn,' said another.

'No spear can pierce his coat,' said a third.

'He hunts the wild asses of the desert,' said a fourth.

'And princes, when he can get them,' said a fifth.

All these five were old, old men. But the sixth was older still.

'I've heard the Iron Lion,' he muttered. 'When I was young and daring I went to the foot of his valley, and I heard his voice.'

'Was it a mighty roar?' said Mustapha.

'More like a mighty yawn,' said the old man, and fell asleep.

The Iron Lion lay at the head of his valley. The sun was high, and the rust-red rocks seemed to bounce and shimmer in the heat. There was no wind, not a lizard scuttled. The drear hills baked in silence. Then, through the silence, came a noise and the Iron Lion pricked up his huge ears.

'Ah well,' he said, 'it's something to do. Here comes another of them. Silly brave nincompoops, but they are a change from donkeys. There've been

41

a lot of them this year for some reason.'

He talked to himself because there was no-one else. His voice was deeper than drums, and from down in the valley it sounded like roaring. Or yawning. The Iron Lion crouched. He knew by the sound of the hooves how far away the prince was, how soon the visor would snap down and the spurs begin to urge the horse to a gallop while the lance lowered for the final, impossible charge. The Iron Lion didn't like lances. They tickled.

But these hooves never changed their beat. They came at an easy pace around all the windings.

'Canny one,' said the Iron Lion and tensed his muscles. The hoofbeats reached the last corner. The Iron Lion sprang.

He sprang straight up in the air, in his effort not to spring forward, and landed with a jolt that shook the hills. Then he watched, puzzled, as the big dappled horse suddenly kicked, and the clown, who had been sitting facing its tail, shot into the air, did a double somersault, and landed the right way around. But the horse had chosen that moment to kneel with its front legs so the clown slid down its back like a child down a chute, rolled through twenty somersaults right to the Iron Lion's feet, and stood up and bowed with ridiculous gravity.

The Iron Lion roared. The roars were laughter,

but no less frightening for that.

You have to be a brave man, and a braver horse, to go through all your circus tricks in front of a lion as big as a barn, whose laughter thunders out of a mouth like a cave where the wet, red tongue, wide as a Sultan's mattress, lolls and flops between yellow teeth. Dapple and Mustapha did every trick they knew, and then did them all over again. Some of them were not so good without the custard pies, but the lion didn't mind. He laughed until he started to hiccup. Mustapha and Dapple rested and waited for the hiccups to stop.

'Thank you,' boomed the lion at last. 'Thank you very much. Now come here and sit on my paw and tell me about the great world, which I shall never see.'

So Mustapha scrambled onto the paw and settled himself as comfortably as he could, considering it was like sitting in a box of four-inch nails, and he told the lion about all the places and things he had seen in his year of travelling about with the circus. He told him about the slave fleets of Tyre, setting off into the sunset with the deep slave voices singing from ship to sad ship. He told him about the metal-beating city of Askelon, where the hammers of the smiths stop neither by night or day and where rich people go out into the country for

picnics, taking servants to beat gongs in case they should go mad with silence. And he told him about the raft towns of the Nile, where the people keep crocodiles instead of watchdogs. And he told him about Baghdad, that rich and wonderful city, whose richest jewel was Yasmin.

'I shall never see her,' growled the lion, and a vast tear flopped from his eyelid to his other paw.

'Now look what you've done!' he roared. 'I've a good mind to gobble you up after all. Dry me before I *rust.*'

Mustapha ran to his saddlebags, fetched his blanket, and started to scrub at the harsh pelt.

'I didn't realize you could rust,' he said.

'Why else do you think I live in this horrible valley? These are the Red Hills, where no rain ever falls. Don't you know any geography? If I get rained on my coat will rust away and then any tin-pot prince can kill me. Or a commoner, even. With a pitchfork.'

Mustapha rubbed in silence until his blanket was in shreds, but the rasping fur was dry.

'As a matter of fact,' he said, 'I've got stuff called oil in my saddlebags which stops iron rusting even if it gets wet.'

'Don't make fun of my afflictions,' said the lion.

'I could oil a little of your fur, and then wet it

45

where it doesn't show. Then we could look in the morning and see if it's worked.'

So they oiled and wetted a tiny patch on the inner side of the lion's paw. That night they all three sat round a fire while Mustapha told the lion more about the enormous world.

Next morning he was awakened by earthquakes and avalanches. The lion was prancing around the hilltops bellowing, 'It worked! It worked! I shall see the world!' Each time he landed there was either an avalanche or an earthquake.

The next two days were tedious for Mustapha, as you can imagine if ever you have tried to oil an animal as big as a barn who can't stand still for excitement. The Iron Lion couldn't decide what he was going to do first after he left the Last Desert. He wanted to learn to swim. He wanted to go to Africa and see if he could eat an elephant in one mouthful. He had a fancy to go to Askelon and get the smiths to make him an iron hat. He wanted to go and bite the top off the highest mountain in the world so that it wasn't the highest mountain any more. And he wanted to go to Baghdad, to see Yasmin.

'As a matter of fact,' said Mustapha, 'that's what would suit me best.'

'Oh, why?'

So Mustapha had to tell him.

'Oh,' said the Iron Lion slowly. 'I wondered why there'd been so many princes. I thought it was something to do with the balance of nature. It's the same with donkeys. Some seasons you have to hunt for hours, and others they just gallop down your throat. Are you a prince too?'

'Yes,' said Mustapha, straightening up from putting the last drop of oil on the last hair of the lion's twitching tail. 'I hope you don't mind the smell of this stuff.'

The lion stood and stretched himself, leg by leg, like a cat getting out of his basket in the morning.

'I like it,' he purred. 'It suits me. It's, well, *leonine.*'

Meanwhile, back at Baghdad, the Prince of Gascony had brought his army and invaded Persia. One by one the Persian armies were sliced and scattered by the terrible, laughing, cruel soldiers of Gascony, until there came a day when the Princess sat again on her jewelled footstool, and the Emperor on his jewelled throne, and the Prince of Gascony stood before them. Otherwise the agate courtyard was empty. All the nobles had fled with their ladies, and the Prince's soldiers now guarded the gate. The Prince twirled his blond moustache.

'Now, my proud beauty,' he cried. 'Once again you have a choice before you. Either you will marry me, or I will chop your father into little pieces.'

'My dear,' whispered the Emperor, 'I fear you may have to accept the offer of this rather uncouth young man.'

Then Yasmin stood and answered the Prince, clear and cold.

'Since His Highness does me the honour of this elegant proposal,' she began, and stopped because the Prince was frowning. There was a noise, a roar, and screams. A blow on the gates like a battering ram. Now the two towers beside the gates were quivering, leaning, falling in a thunder of smoking brick dust as the gate itself was whisked aside.

And there, looming above the smoke, came the Iron Lion of Ferdustan.

The Prince of Gascony shouted his battle cry, drew his sword, and dashed at the monster, who gobbled him up.

But the Princess was looking at the man on the lion's shoulders. He wore the shining armour of a noble kingdom, and she saw in a glance that he was handsome. He must be brave to ride such a beast and clever to have brought it. She guessed he was kind.

The young man slid from the lion's back and the lion went off to chase Gascons. Mustapha introduced himself, and the Emperor was gracious enough to pretend to remember his father. And then Mustapha and Yasmin went walking for a long hour through the peacock gardens.

That evening Mustapha and Dapple went down into the city to visit a friend.

'Ach!' cried Herman. 'You have come back. You dis prince nonsense have forgotten! Ah, how we missed you. Your vages, your vages!'

'Herman,' said Mustapha, 'I have met someone who wants to work in your circus.'

'Ach, mein friend, I cannot anodder clown afford!'

'He's not a clown, and he doesn't want wages. All he wants is to see the world.'

And he took Herman out to where the Iron Lion stood colossal in the dusk. Herman threw his arms wide and hugged Mustapha and kissed him on both cheeks.

'Ach, vot an attraction!' he cried. 'Now mine der biggest *big* circus in der vorld vill be!'

And that is really the end of the story. They all lived happily ever after, but happiest of all was the Iron Lion, who did all the things he had always wanted to do, and then, when the circus closed for the hot weather, came back to Baghdad and lay panting in the orange grove below the palace wall, while Mustapha's and Yasmin's children, and later on their grandchildren, tore hundreds of pairs of trousers by sliding down his shanks.

This story is by Peter Dickinson.

Linnet's Story

It was Christmas Eve. There had been snow, then a dripping thaw that had filled the river, followed by a sudden hard frost. The trees dangled with icicles that tinkled like Japanese bells. The eaves were jagged with ice daggers. The ground was hard like glazed rock, the moat frozen. Toby and Alexander, with their mother, had gone on foot to Midnight Mass at the big church in Penny Soaky across the river. The little church in this village belonged to what Linnet called the preachies, who did not celebrate Midnight Mass. The family had gone on foot because the road was too slippery for horses, the ruts too hard for a coach. Linnet could not walk so far, so she was put to bed and the grandmother sat downstairs alone. Linnet took Orlando, her little black and white curly dog, to bed with her.

She had a little spruce tree in her bedroom – it

51

was her own idea – for the birds. On such a cold night her tame birds had come in to sleep in its branches. They were curled up with their heads under their wings. The tits were balls of blue, or primrose-green; the robins red; the chaffinches pink. Linnet had put a crystal star on top. It glittered among the shadows in the candlelight.

As she lay in bed she heard the wind singing through the icicles outside. It was an eerie sound that made her think of the enormous silence of the country across which it blew. Every now and then an icicle broke off with a sharp crack.

Linnet lay and listened, thinking of her mother and her two brothers walking along the field paths in the brilliant moonlight with their black shadows following under their feet. If she listened for the outside noises she could hear the water going through the water gates and over the weir. There was no flood, but a deep, strong current. She could hear occasionally the owls and the desolate herons. Once she heard a fox bark. Inside her room perhaps one of the birds shifted and chirped softly in its sleep. She could hear Orlando breathing into his own fur. She could hear the candle flame fluttering like a little flag. It was all so very quiet.

Presently she heard something else, something very strange. Outside on the ice-hard ground there were footsteps that could be nothing and nobody that she knew, not Boggis's hobnailed boots, not her grandmother nor the quick young maid, not a horse! She was not frightened, she was simply certain that it did not belong to the everyday world. Orlando woke up and listened. Linnet could feel his tail softly beating against her ribs.

She got out of bed, wrapping herself in the cover so that she looked like the Russian doll, then she opened the window and leant out. Orlando stood beside her with his paws on the window sill. She could distinctly hear the steps, heavy but soft, coming along the side of the house. The wind was like a knife against her cheek and all the stars twinkled with cold. Orlando's reassuring tail was still wagging against her.

Out into the moonlight came St. Christopher himself, huge and gentle with his head among the stars, taking the stone Child on his shoulders to Midnight Mass. As they went past, Orlando lifted his chin and gave a little cry, and from the stables came a quiet whinny. All the birds in the spruce tree woke up and flew out of the window, circling round St. Christopher with excited calls. The stone giant strode across the lawns with his bare feet and soon came to the river. At the edge there was thin, loose ice that shivered like a window-pane as he

stepped in. The water rushed round his legs and the reflection of the moon was torn to wet ribbons. The stream crept up to his waist and, as he still went on, to his armpits. When it looked as if he could go no farther Linnet heard a child's voice singing gaily. The sound was torn and scattered by the wind as the moon's reflection had been by the water, but she recognized the song as it came in snatches.

> To-morrow shall be my dancing day
> I would my true love did so chance
> To see the legend of my play
> To call my true love to the dance.
> Sing O my love, O my love, my love, my
>   love,
> This have I done for my true love.

As the Child sang, it clutched St. Christopher by the hair to hold him firmly.

St. Christopher felt his way carefully foot by foot, through the deepest part and came out safely on the other side. Linnet saw him striding away across the meadows. The birds returned, coming in one by one past her head at the open window and chattering as they settled down again on the tree.

When St. Christopher was out of sight Linnet

realized that it was cold. She also remembered that she had got into bed without saying her prayers. She said them now, and Orlando lay on her feet and kept them warm till she had finished. Then she got into bed again and before long the bells rang out for midnight, and it was Christmas morning. When the boys came back she told them what she had seen. Alexander said he too had seen St. Christopher kneeling among the tombstones outside the church in the shadow of a big cypress tree. He thought nobody else had noticed.

Of course they rushed out first thing in the morning to look, and found St. Christopher in his place as usual with icicles all over him, but the sun was falling on the stone Child and the hand that it held up looked almost pink.

This story is by Lucy Boston.

The house at Green Knowe is based on Lucy Boston's real home, The Manor at Hemingford Grey near Huntingdon. The house and gardens, which contain Lucy Boston's topiary coronation and chess pieces, are open to visitors all year round, by prior appointment.

The Brollachan whose Mother was a Fuath

This is a story about a Brollachan.

You will now want to know what a Brollachan is and I will tell you. A Brollachan is a dark, splodgy, shapeless thing. It has two red eyes, an enormous mouth and absolutely nothing else whatsoever. A Brollachan has no bones and no stomach and no nose. It has no arms and no legs and no feet and no toes and therefore no toenails. And it has no hair. There is probably nothing with less hair than a Brollachan.

A Brollachan, then, is just a squashy and quite frightening blob which rolls about the place. But though it has no shape of its own a Brollachan can take on the shape of things that it meets. A Brollachan lying on a table, for example, might become table-shaped or a Brollachan looking at a round Dutch cheese could become cheese-shaped if it wished. And though it cannot really think it can hear a little through its bulges and it can certainly feel.

The Brollachan that this story is about lived in a house beside a swampy pond with his mother who was a Fuath. Fuaths are evil and bad-tempered fairies who live near water, so they are often dripping wet. They look almost like ordinary ladies but if you look at them carefully you will find that there is something odd about them. Sometimes they are hollow from behind, and sometimes they have only one nostril.

The Brollachan's mother had a long nose with a black wart on it, whiskery ears, one frightful long tooth and webbed feet. She was a worrier and she was a nagger. She wanted the Brollachan to be more scary and more shapeless than he was. She wanted him to lure people into the swamp by terrifying them with his vile red eyes. She wanted him to bubble disgustingly in the mud at the bottom of the pond and she wanted him to speak.

'Say "Mummy",' she would yell at him, 'go on, say it. Say "Mummy".'

But the Brollachan couldn't say 'Mummy'. He couldn't say anything. His mouth was big but he used it for eating, not for talking. So he would roll away sadly and suck in a large turnip or a dead rat or a ham-bone and you would see them – the turnip or the rat or the ham-bone – lying inside him sort of glowing a little until they gradually became part of the Brollachan because that is what happens to the things that Brollachans eat.

All day long the Brollachan's mother followed him about flapping a wet cloth at the furniture and dripping water on him.

'I don't know what will become of you, Brollachan. Why aren't you outside drowning someone? Why are you sitting in that bucket? Why don't you do something with your life. And why don't you say "Mummy"?'

The Brollachan tried hard to please her. But however wide he opened his mouth, all that came out was a kind of gulp or a sort of glucking noise.

Sometimes the Brollachan's mother invited her friends round; ladies like Black Annis who was a cannibal witch with a blue face or the Hag of the Dribble who was covered all over in grey slime, and then she would start:

'You don't know how I worry about him,' she would say to these ladies, prodding the Brollachan with her webbed foot as he lay politely on the floor. 'I can't sleep for worrying about him. He's so backward; he doesn't even try to frighten people into fits. And he won't say "Mummy"!'

'You should punish him,' said the cannibal witch, burping rudely because she always swallowed people whole and this gave her wind. 'Make him kneel on dried peas – nothing more painful than that!'

Which was not only a cruel but a silly thing to say since the Brollachan did not have any knees.

One day the Brollachan and his mother went for a walk in the forest. The Brollachan liked the forest very much. It was not wet like the swamp where he lived and the leaves felt pleasantly tickly under his body. He stretched himself out more and more and became bush-shaped, then tree-shaped and then just Brollachan-shaped but extra large. He felt happy and he felt free.

But the Brollachan's mother was still talking. 'Why don't you learn the names of the trees, Brollachan?' she said. 'Why don't you at least try to give off an evil mist? There's a Brollachan in the next valley who has a whole village gibbering with fright every time he shows himself. *And* he can say "Mummy"!'

After a while the Brollachan rolled away between the trees and he rolled and he rolled and he rolled until he was quite a way from his mother.

The Brollachan's mother did not notice this at first because she was so busy talking. 'It's all right for you,' she said, 'you can't have a stomach-ache from worrying because you haven't got a stomach. You can't have a headache from worrying because you haven't got a head. You can't – Brollachan, where are you? Brollachan, come here at once. I'm talking to you. How dare you hide from your mother! I can see your vile red eyes behind that tree. I know you're just pretending to be that smelly toadstool. Now come to your mummy, Brollachan; come at once!'

But the Brollachan was a long, long way away and he was well and truly lost. He rolled on, however, until he came to a little wooden house in a clearing and because he was very tired by now, he oozed through the crack under the door and went inside.

It was a very nice house. There was a fire in the grate and a painted stool and a rocking chair in one corner. In the rocking chair, fast asleep, sat an old man with a kind face and a long white beard. Everything was quiet and everything was dry and the Brollachan liked it very much. And becoming more or less the shape of the hearthrug he lay down by the fire, closed his vile red eyes and fell asleep.

He slept for one hour and he slept for two while outside in the forest his mother, the Fuath, roared about on her webbed feet, searching and scolding and calling him. Goodness knows how long he might have gone on sleeping but just then a burning coal fell out of the fireplace and landed on one of the Brollachan's bulges.

Now the Brollachan couldn't talk but he could scream – and scream he did!

Everything then happened at once. The old man woke, saw that there was a Brollachan on his hearthrug and jumped from his rocking chair. The Brollachan's mother heard the scream and rushed in at the front door, dripping and shouting as she came.

'What's happened to you, Brollachan? How did

you get here? Who hurt you? Has that nasty old
man hurt you? Have you hurt my Brollachan, you
stupid old man? Because if you have I'll turn
you into a bat with bunions. I'll turn you into an
eel with earache. I'll claw you into strips of raw
beef, I'll make newts come out of your nostrils,
I'll . . .'

On and on she raged. The old man did not know how to bear so much noise. He took his long white beard and stuffed the left half of it into his left ear and the right half of it into his right ear but still he could hear the Fuath's voice. Feeling quite desperate he got a broom and tried to shoo the Fuath out of doors.

But the Fuath would not be shushed and she would not be shooed. She just dripped and she threatened and she *talked*.

The Brollachan by now was very upset. His burn did not hurt any longer but he felt that things were not as they should be. His red eyes were wide with worry and his shapeless darkness shivered at all this unpleasantness. What he wanted more than anything was to make things all right.

So he made himself very big and he opened his mouth and he went right up to his mother, who was still talking and scolding and waving her arms. If only he could do it! If only he could do the thing she wanted so much! Wider he opened his mouth and wider . . . and closer he went to his mother and closer . . . and harder he tried and harder . . . harder than he had ever tried in his whole life.

And then at last he did it. He actually did it!

'MUMMY!' said the Brollachan. 'MUM – gluck – gulp!'

Then he stopped. His mother was not there.

The Brollachan was puzzled. He looked under the stool and behind the door but there was no sign of her. But though he was puzzled, he was not worried. He felt very close to his mother. And because it made him tired to be so clever he lay down again – but further from the fire – and fell asleep.

The old man took half his beard out of his right ear and half his beard out of his left ear and came over to have a look. He could see the Brollachan's mother inside the Brollachan as clear as clear. He could even see the wart on the end of her nose. She was still talking and talking and talking but Brollachans are soundproof so he couldn't hear a thing.

So he smiled and nodded at the Brollachan as if to say, yes, you can stay, and went back to his rocking chair. The next day he made a fireguard so that the Brollachan wouldn't get burnt. And then he and the Brollachan lived together very happily. Because both of them had said all they were ever going to say and each was happy to let the other be the kind of person that he was.

This story is by Eva Ibbotson.

The Dolphin Rider

This is the tale of Arion. He was a very talented young man who asked Apollo, the god of music, to teach him the lyre. Apollo was so amused by this bold request, which no-one in the world had dared to make before, that he taught Arion to play the lyre most beautifully.

Now Arion lived in a city near the sea called Corinth. He was a bold, adventure-loving youth, and wanted very much to travel. But when he was a child an oracle, foretelling the future, had said, 'Avoid the sea. For no ship will bring you back from any voyage you make.' Arion's parents believed this, and made him stay at home.

But the boy grew more restless every day. He would go down to the harbour and watch the ships scudding out to the open sea, their sails spread to the wind. When he saw this he felt full of longing for far places. He would unsling his lyre and sing a song of ships and storms and castaways . . . of giants and cannibals and sea-monsters, and all the adventures he had dreamed of.

His song was so beautiful that dolphins rose to the surface to listen. They sat there in the water, balancing themselves on their tails, listening. Sometimes they wept great salt tears. When Arion stopped singing, they clapped their flippers, shouting, 'Bravo! Bravo! More . . . more!' and he would have to sing again. Often he sang to them all night long. And when the stars paled he could see giant shadows gliding nearby – swordfish and sharks, devilfish and giant turtles, which had risen from the depths, not for an easy meal, but to listen to the enchanting sounds he was making.

Then, for his twentieth birthday, Apollo gave Arion a golden lyre. The youth was eager to try it out at the great music festival held in Sicily.

'Oracles and soothsayers are gloomy by nature,' he told himself. 'How often do they tell you anything happy? They try to scare you so that you'll come back and pay them again, hoping to hear something better. Anyway, that's what I choose to believe, for I must see the world no matter what happens.'

So Arion took his lyre and set sail for Sicily. He played and sang so beautifully in the festival that the audience went mad with delight. They heaped gifts upon him – a jewelled sword, a suit of silver armour, an ivory bow and quiver of bronze-tipped arrows, and a fat bag of gold. Arion was so happy that he forgot all about the prophecy. In his eagerness to get home and tell about his triumphs, he took the first ship back to Corinth, although the captain was a huge, ugly, dangerous-looking fellow, with an even uglier crew.

On the first afternoon out, Arion was sitting in the bow, gazing at the purple sea, when the captain strode up and said, 'Pity - you're so young to die.'

'Am I to die young?' Arion asked.

'Yes.'

'Are you sure?'

'Absolutely certain.'

'What makes you so sure?'

'Because I'm going to kill you.'

'That does seem a pity,' said Arion. 'When is this sad event to take place?'

'Soon. In fact, immediately.'

'But why? What have I done?'

'Something foolish. You let yourself become the owner of a treasure that I must have — that jewelled sword, the silver armour, not to mention that delicious, fat bag of gold. You should never show things like that to thieves.

68

'Why can't you take what you want without killing me?'

'Too big a risk, my boy. You might complain to the king about being robbed, and that would be very dangerous for us. So you have to go. I'm sure you understand.'

'I see you've thought the matter over carefully,' said Arion. 'Well, I have only this to ask: let me sing a last song before I die.'

At the music festival, Arion had composed a song of praise to be sung on special occasions. And he sang it now – praising first Apollo, who had taught him music, then old Neptune, master of the sea. He sang praise to the sea itself and those who dwell there – the gulls and ocean nymphs and gliding fish. He sang to the magic changefulness of the waters, which put on different colours as the sun climbs and sinks.

So singing, Arion leaped from the bow of the ship, lyre in hand, and plunged into the sea.

He had sung so beautifully that the creatures of the deep had swum up to hear him. Among them was a school of dolphins. The largest one quickly dived, then rose to the surface, lifting Arion on his back.

'Thank you, friend,' said Arion.

'A poor favour to return for such heavenly

music,' said the dolphin as he swam away with Arion on his back.

The other dolphins danced along on the water, as Arion played. They swam very swiftly and brought Arion to Corinth a day before the ship was due. He went immediately to his friend, Periander, king of Corinth, and told him his story. Then he took the king down to the waterfront to introduce him to the dolphin that had saved his life. The dolphin, who had become very fond of Arion, longed to stay with him in Corinth. So the king had the river dammed up to make a giant pool on the palace grounds, and there the dolphin stayed when he wished to visit Arion.

When the thieves' ship arrived in port, captain and crew were seized by the king's guard and taken to the castle. Arion stayed hidden.

'Why have you taken us captive, oh King?' said the captain. 'We are peaceable law-abiding sailors.'

'My friend Arion took passage on your ship!' roared the king. 'Where is he? What have you done with him?'

'Poor lad,' said the captain. 'He was quite mad. He was on deck singing to himself one day, and then suddenly jumped overboard. We put out a small boat, circled the spot for hours. We couldn't find a trace. Sharks probably. Sea's full of them there.'

'And what do you do to a man-eating shark when you catch him?' asked the king.

'Kill him, of course,' said the captain. 'We can't let them swim free and eat other sailors.'

'A noble sentiment,' said Arion, stepping out of his hiding place. 'That's exactly what we do to two-legged sharks in Corinth.'

So the captain and his crew were taken out and hanged. The ship was searched and Arion found all that had been taken from him. He insisted on dividing the gifts with the king. When Periander protested, Arion laughed and said: 'Treasures are trouble. You're a king and can handle them. But I'm a minstrel and must travel light.'

And all his life Arion sang songs of praise. His music grew in power and beauty until people said he was a second Orpheus. When he died Apollo set him in the sky – and his lyre, and the dolphin too. They shine in the night sky still, the stars of constellations we still call the Lyre and the Dolphin.

This story is by Bernard Evslin.

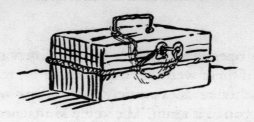

Humblepuppy

Our house was furnished mainly from auction sales. When you buy furniture that way you get a lot of extra things besides the particular piece that you were after, since the stuff is sold in lots: Lot 13, two Persian rugs, a set of golf-clubs, a sewing-machine, a walnut radio-cabinet, and a plinth.

It was in this way that I acquired a tin deedbox, which came with two coal-scuttles and a broom cupboard. The deedbox is solid metal, painted black, big as a medium-sized suitcase. When I first brought it home I put it in my study, planning to use it as a kind of filing-cabinet for old typescripts. I had gone into the kitchen, and was busy arranging the brooms in their new home, when I heard a loud thumping coming from the direction of the study.

I went back, thinking that a bird must have flown through the window; no bird, but the banging seemed to be inside the deedbox. I had

73

already opened it as soon as it was in my possession, to see if there were any diamonds or bearer bonds worth thousands of pounds inside (there weren't), but I opened it again. The key was attached to the handle by a thin chain. There was nothing inside. I shut it. The banging started again. I opened it.

Still nothing inside.

Well, this was broad daylight, two o'clock on Thursday afternoon, people going past in the road outside and a radio schools programme chatting away to itself in the next room. It was not a ghostly kind of time, so I put my hand into the empty box and moved it about.

Something shrank away from my hand. I heard a faint, scared whimper. It could almost have been my own, but wasn't. Knowing that someone – something? – else was afraid too put heart into me. Exploring carefully and gently around the interior of the box I felt the contour of a small, bony, warm, trembling body with big awkward feet, and silky dangling ears, and a cold nose that, when I found it, nudged for a moment anxiously but trustingly into the palm of my hand. So I knelt down, put the other hand into the box as well, cupped them under a thin little ribby chest, and lifted out Humblepuppy.

He was quite light.

I couldn't see him, but I could hear his faint inquiring whimper, and I could hear his toenails scratch on the floorboards.

Just at that moment the cat, Taffy, came in.

Taffy has a lot of character. Every cat has a lot of character, but Taffy has more than most, all of it inconvenient. For instance, although he is very sociable, and longs for company, he just despises company in the form of dogs. The mere sound of a dog barking two streets away is enough to make his fur stand up like a porcupine's quills and his tail swell like a mushroom cloud.

Which it did the instant he saw Humblepuppy.

Now here is the interesting thing. I could feel and hear Humblepuppy, but couldn't see him; Taffy, apparently, could see and smell him, but couldn't feel him. We soon discovered this. For Taffy, sinking into a low, gladiator's crouch, letting out all the time a fearsome throaty wauling like a bagpipe revving up its drone, inched his way along to where Humblepuppy huddled trembling by my left foot, and then dealt him what ought to have been a swinging right-handed clip on the ear. 'Get out of my house, you filthy little canine scum!' was what he was plainly intending to convey.

But the swipe failed to connect; instead it landed on my shin. I've never seen a cat so astonished. It was like watching a kitten meet itself for the first time in a looking-glass. Taffy ran round to the back of where Humblepuppy was sitting; felt; smelt; poked gingerly with a paw; leapt back nervously; crept forward again. All the time Humblepuppy just sat, trembling a little, giving out this faint beseeching sound that meant: 'I'm only a poor little mongrel without a smidgeon of harm in me. *Please* don't do anything nasty! I don't even know how I came here.'

It certainly was a puzzle how he had come. I rang the auctioneers (after shutting Taffy *out* and Humblepuppy *in* to the study with a bowl of water and a handful of Boniebisk, Taffy's favourite breakfast food).

The auctioneers told me that Lot 12, Deedbox, coal-scuttles and broom cupboard, had come from Riverland Rectory, where Mr Smythe, the old rector, had lately died aged ninety. Had he ever possessed a dog, or a puppy? They couldn't say; they had merely received instructions from a firm of lawyers to sell the furniture.

I never did discover how poor little Humblepuppy's ghost got into that deedbox. Maybe he was shut in by mistake, long ago, and suffocated; maybe some callous Victorian gardener dropped him, box and all, into a river, and the box was later found and fished out.

Anyway, and whatever had happened in the past, now that Humblepuppy had come out of his box, he was very pleased with the turn his affairs had taken, ready to be grateful and affectionate. As I sat typing I'd often hear a patter-patter, and feel his small chin fit itself comfortably over my foot, ears dangling. Goodness knows what kind of a mixture he was; something between a spaniel and a terrier, I'd guess. In the evening, watching television or sitting by the fire, one would suddenly find his warm weight leaning against one's leg. (He didn't put on a lot of weight while he was with us, but his bony little ribs filled out a bit.)

For the first few weeks we had a lot of trouble with Taffy, who was very surly over the whole business and blamed me bitterly for not getting rid of this low-class intruder. But Humblepuppy was extremely placating, got back into his deedbox whenever the atmosphere became too volcanic, and did his very best not to be a nuisance.

By and by Taffy thawed. As I've said, he is really a very sociable cat. Although quite old, seventy cat years, he dearly likes cheerful company, and generally has some young cat friend who comes to play with him, either in the house or the garden. In the last few years we've had Whisky, the black and

white pub cat, who used to sit washing the smell of fish-and-chips off his fur under the dripping tap in our kitchen sink; Tetanus, the hairdresser's thickset black, who took a fancy to sleep on top of our china-cupboard every night all one winter, and used to startle me very much by jumping down heavily on to my shoulder as I made the breakfast coffee; Sweet Charity, a little grey Persian who came to a sad end under the wheels of a police-car; Charity's grey-and-white stripy cousin Fred, whose owners presently moved from next door to another part of the town.

It was soon after Fred's departure that Humblepuppy arrived, and from my point of view he couldn't have been more welcome. Taffy missed Fred badly, and expected *me* to play with him instead; it was sad to see this large elderly tabby rushing hopefully up and down the stairs after breakfast, or hiding behind the armchair and jumping out on to nobody; or howling, howling, howling at me until I escorted him out into the garden, where he'd rush to the lavender-bush which had been the traditional hiding-place of Whisky, Tetanus, Charity, and Fred in succession. Cats have their habits and histories, just the same as humans.

So sometimes, on a working morning, I'd be at

my wits' end, almost on the point of going across the town to our ex-neighbours, ringing their bell, and saying, 'Please can Fred come and play?' 'Specially on a rainy, uninviting day when Taffy was pacing gloomily about the house with drooping head and switching tail, grumbling about the weather and the lack of company, and blaming me for both.

Humblepuppy's arrival changed all that.

At first Taffy considered it necessary to police him, and that kept him fully occupied for hours. He'd sit on guard by the deedbox till Humblepuppy woke up in the morning, and then he'd follow officiously all over the house, wherever the visitor went. Humblepuppy was slow and cautious in his explorations, but by degrees he picked up courage and found his way into every corner. He never once made a puddle; he learned to use Taffy's cat-flap and go out into the garden, though he was always more timid outside and would scamper for home at any loud noise. Planes and cars terrified him, he never became used to them; which made me still more certain that he had been in that deedbox for a long, long time, since before such things were invented.

Presently he learned, or Taffy taught him, to hide in the lavender-bush like Whisky, Charity,

Tetanus, and Fred; and the two of them used to play their own ghostly version of touch-last for hours on end while I got on with my typing.

When visitors came, Humblepuppy always retired to his deedbox; he was decidedly scared of strangers; which made his behaviour with Mr Manningham, the new rector of Riverland, all the more surprising.

I was dying to learn anything I could of the old rectory's history, so I'd invited Mr Manningham to tea.

He was a thin, gentle, quiet man, who had done missionary work in the Far East and fell ill and had to come back to England. He seemed a little sad and lonely; said he still missed his Far East friends and work. I liked him. He told me that for a large part of the nineteenth century the Riverland living had belonged to a parson called Swannett, the Reverend Timothy Swannett, who lived to a great age and had ten children.

'He was a great-uncle of mine, as a matter of fact. But why do you want to know all this?' Mr Manningham asked. His long thin arm hung over the side of his chair; absently he moved his hand sideways and remarked, 'I didn't notice that you had a puppy.' Then he looked down and said, 'Oh!'

81

'He's never come out for a stranger before,' I said.

Taffy, who maintains a civil reserve with visitors, sat motionless on the nightstore heater, eyes slitted, sphinx-like.

Humblepuppy climbed invisibly onto Mr Manningham's lap.

We agreed that the new rector probably carried a familiar smell of his rectory with him; or possibly he reminded Humblepuppy of his great-uncle, the Rev. Swannett.

Anyway, after that, Humblepuppy always came scampering joyfully out if Mr Manningham dropped in to tea, so of course I thought of the rector when summer holiday time came round.

During the summer holidays we lend our house and cat to a lady publisher and her mother who are devoted to cats and think it a privilege to look after Taffy and spoil him. He is always amazingly overweight when we get back. But the old lady has an allergy to dogs, and is frightened of them too; it was plainly out of the question that she should be expected to share her summer holiday with the ghost of a puppy.

So I asked Mr Manningham if he'd be prepared to take Humblepuppy as a boarder, since it didn't seem a case for the usual kind of boarding-kennels;

he said he'd be delighted.

I drove Humblepuppy out to Riverland in his deedbox; he was rather miserable on the drive, but luckily it is not far. Mr Manningham came out into the garden to meet us. We put the box down on the lawn and opened it.

I've never heard a puppy so wildly excited. Often I'd been sorry that I couldn't see Humblepuppy, but I was never sorrier than on that afternoon, as we heard him rushing from tree to familiar tree, barking joyously, dashing through the orchard grass – you could see it divide as he whizzed along – coming back to bounce up against us, all damp and earthy and smelling of leaves.

'He's going to be happy with you, all right,' I said, and Mr Manningham's grey, lined face crinkled into its thoughtful smile as he said, 'It's the place more than me, I think.'

Well, it was both of them, really.

After the holiday, I went to collect Humblepuppy, leaving Taffy haughty and stand-offish, sniffing our cases. It always takes him a long time to forgive us for going away.

Mr Manningham had a bit of a cold and was sitting by the fire in his study, wrapped in a Shetland rug. Humblepuppy was on his knee. I could hear the little dog's tail thump against the arm

of the chair when I walked in, but he didn't get down to greet me. He stayed in Mr Manningham's lap.

'So you've come to take back my boarder,' Mr Manningham said.

There was nothing in the least strained about his voice or smile but – I just hadn't the heart to take back Humblepuppy. I put my hand down, found his soft wrinkly forehead, rumpled it a bit, and said,

'Well – I was sort of wondering: our spoilt old cat seems to have got used to being on his own again; I was wondering whether – by any chance – you'd feel like keeping him?'

Mr Manningham's face lit up. He didn't speak for a minute; then he put a gentle hand down to find the small head, and rubbed a finger along Humblepuppy's chin.

'Well,' he said. He cleared his throat. 'Of course, if you're *quite* sure —'

'Quite sure.' My throat needed clearing too.

'I hope you won't catch my cold,' Mr Manningham said. I shook my head and said, 'I'll drop in to see if you're better in a day or two,' and went off and left them together.

Poor Taffy was pretty glum over the loss of his playmate for several weeks; we had two hours' purgatory every morning after breakfast while he hunted for Humblepuppy high and low. But gradually the memory faded and, thank goodness, now he has found a new friend, Little Grey Furry, a nephew, cousin or other relative of Charity and Fred. Little Grey Furry has learned to play hide-and-seek in the lavender-bush, and to use our cat-flap, and clean up whatever's in Taffy's food bowl, so all is well in that department.

But I still miss Humblepuppy. I miss his cold nose exploring the palm of my hand, as I sit thinking, in the middle of a page, and his warm weight leaning against my knee as he watches the commercials. And the scritch-scratch of his toenails on the dining-room floor and the flump, flump, as he comes downstairs, and the small hollow in a cushion as he settles down with a sigh.

Oh well. I'll get over it, just as Taffy has. But I was wondering about putting an ad. into *Our Dogs* or *Pets' Monthly:* Wanted, ghost of mongrel puppy. Warm welcome, loving home. Any reasonable price paid.

It might be worth a try.

This story is by Joan Aiken.

The Tough Guys

We are the Peg Men, and we are the toughest kids at Mill Road Primary School.

We let everybody know that we are tough. We put PEG MEN RULE OK on the shelters down on the promenade and BEWARE OF THE PEG MEN on the bike shed and THIS IS PEGLAND on the toilets and KEEP OUT BY ORDER OF THE PEG MEN on Logan's wall, and everybody is scared of us.

Henry Peg is the leader of the Peg Men, and what he says goes. I'm Sam Ball, and I'm a Peg Man and so is my brother Leo. The other Peg Man is Henry's little brother Philip. Mrs Peg calls him Philip but we all call him Piglet, because he squeaks like one. There aren't any other boys down Keel Point Lane, so there aren't any other Peg Men. Henry Peg won't let girls in it, because he says girls are soppy, even Rosie Mitten.

We didn't know about Rosie Mitten until the afternoon of the Keel Point Harbour Sports Day. All the big kids from up the Main Street came, and they were in the swimming and the diving and the Pull-The-Punt. Henry Peg's sister Lily Peg was Harbour Queen and she wandered round in her bathing costume turning blue, because it was cold. It always is cold, on Harbour Sports Day.

We weren't in the swimming or the diving or things like that, because we are not allowed out of our depth, but we entered almost everything else.

We were in the Sack Race and the Three Legger and the Egg-and-Spoon and the Trampoline Championship. I won that because I am good at bouncing.

It was my mum who spotted Rosie Mitten in her soppy yellow dress, with her soppy glasses and her soppy plaits. My mum went over to Rosie and said how nice it was to see a new face at Keel Point and how she really mustn't miss out on all the fun because she didn't know anyone, and wouldn't she like to join in the pillow fight?

Any sensible girl would have said 'No' because girls get bashed in pillow fights, but Rosie Mitten said 'Yes', and she thanked my mum very much for asking her. My mum told Mrs Peg what a nice polite little girl Rosie Mitten was.

'I'm not fighting *girls*!' Henry Peg said.

'Yes you are, if the draw works out that way!' said Mrs Peg.

We do the pillow fight on a greasy pole, stuck out over the water. My dad and Henry Peg's dad and the harbour master and Mr Watts from our school got the pole fixed in position on the pier with ropes holding it between the harbour rail and a bollard. Then I got on the pole with Henry Peg and Leo with gooey handfuls of grease and we greased it right up to the end so that it was dead slippery, and then we shoved each other in.

SPLASH!

SPLASH!

SPLOSH!

The splosh was Henry Peg, who was showing off because he can do twenty strokes. He didn't have to swim twenty strokes, because it was only up to his belly button, but he wanted to show off anyway. He put his hands on the bottom and kicked his feet and pretended to swim lots of strokes so that all the grown-ups would think he was a real channel swimmer.

Walter Bruce dive-bombed him, and all Walter's mates cheered. They are from the estate at Big Road. They call themselves the Big Road Eagles and they are our Deadly Enemies. Walter's mum was mad with him and said not to dare do such a thing again to little Henry. I don't think Henry was pleased at being called little.

Mr Watts gave us the soggy pillows to fight with. The pillows were soggy because Walter Bruce had been holding them when he dive-bombed Henry Peg, which is the other reason Mrs Bruce was cross with Walter.

We enjoyed Mrs Bruce being cross, because she waves her arms around like a windmill when she gets mad.

In the Harbour Sports Pillow Fight there is a draw, first of all, to work out who fights who. Then the first two people who are going to fight have to go out on the greasy pole. Somebody chucks them pillows and then they bash crash smash and mash each other with the pillows until somebody falls off. Usually both people fall off, but the first one to hit the water is the loser and the winner goes into the next round.

Henry Peg's sister Lily was the Harbour Queen so they brought her in off her Harbour Queen float to make the draw. They gave her a coat to wear because she was shivery. Then she had to stand up on a wall and pick names out of a blue plastic bucket. The harbour master wrote them up on Mr Watt's old blackboard.

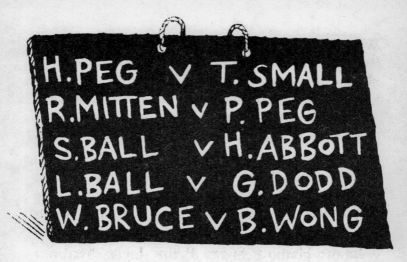

H.PEG ∨ T.SMALL
R.MITTEN ∨ P.PEG
S.BALL ∨ H.ABBOTT
L.BALL ∨ G.DODD
W.BRUCE ∨ B.WONG

'It's a fix!' Henry Peg said. 'That Rosie Mitten got Piglet because he's the smallest one, and she's a girl!'

'Piglet will smash her!' said Leo.

We all thought that Piglet *might,* so long as he didn't fall off the pole first, before the smashing even began. Piglet is small, but he is a Peg Man, and Peg Men are tough!

The rest of the draw was Peg Men against Big Road Eagles, except for Wongy fighting Walter Bruce which was two Eagles against each other. We hoped Wongy would clout Walter, because otherwise we didn't know who was going to stop him. We don't reckon it is fair Walter being in the Eagles, because he is bigger than almost anybody.

We were all on Wongy's side, even though he is an Eagle.

The first fight was H. Peg against T. Small, Peg Men versus Eagles. Henry got his pillow and went out on the pole and absolutely bashed Tom Small till Tom fell in. We all cheered because our side had won!

Then it was Piglet against Rosie Mitten.

'Go on, Piglet!' we shouted. 'Bash her!'

'Give her a bath!' shouted Henry Peg. He didn't shout very loudly in case his mother heard him. She was busy giving beef tea to the shivery Harbour Queen at the time, so she missed it.

Henry Peg went up to Rosie and told her the water was full of gi–normous crabs and she'd better keep her soppy glasses on so that she could look out for them.

Rosie didn't say a thing.

She took her glasses off and put them on the towel my mum had lent her, for drying off after Piglet knocked her into the drink!

That is what we hoped would happen. Soppy Rosie would go KER-SPLOSH! and come up crying!

Piglet put on his fighting face and edged his way along the pole. He was first out. Rosie Mitten waited. She had on a sissy swimming suit with roses on it, just like her name.

Piglet got out to the end of the pole, and settled himself on the greasy bit. He gave us the thumbs up, and nearly fell off!

Rosie Mitten climbed onto the pole.

'Ready?' Mr Watts shouted. 'Give them the pillows.'

It was Walter Bruce who was in charge of pillow chucking. He lobbed Rosie's at her, and Rosie caught it, but when he went to give Piglet *his* pillow, Walter really chucked it hard.

SMACK!

The wet pillow caught Piglet right in the chops.

'Wooooooooo!' went Piglet, and he wobbled on the greasy pole and started to slip round, and the next moment . . .

SPLOSH!

All the Eagles cheered!

Piglet went right under, and when he got his head above the water he didn't even squeak. He just sat there with the water up to his pig-snout, gulping.

'Doesn't count!' said Mr Watts firmly, and he hauled Piglet out of the water, but there was no way Piglet was going out on the pole again.

'Don't make him or he'll cry!' Lily Peg told her mother, and Mrs Peg got hold of Piglet and wrapped him up in Lily's Harbour Queen towel before he could start howling.

'What about me?' Rosie said, climbing back on to the pier.

'You get a walk-over, dear,' said Mr Watts.

'More like a drop-under!' said Tom Small, and all the Eagles started grinning, and making jokes about Peg Men being cry-babies.

Mr Watts took the pillows off Walter after that, but it was too late. It was me next, for the Glory of the Peg Men.

Hugh Abbott, the Big Road Eagle I was fighting, is *very* big. He is as big as Walter Bruce, almost, although he still has a year to go before he goes up to Scouts.

I got him one BIFF – a brilliant Sam Ball Buster Bang!

It was a really good one, and he started to wobble, and I swung again, to give him my Abbott Crusher Pillow Bash, only he cheated. He caught my pillow, and pulled me towards him.

Then . . .

BIFF!

BASH!

BIFF-BIFF-BIFF!

BUFF!

I went over, but I caught his leg on the way

down and he came ker-splosh after me in the biggest ever water bomb at the Harbour Sports.

I lost, because Mr Watts said I hit the water first. Mr Watts said I was cheating because I grabbed him when I was going down.

'Hugh grabbed my pillow first!' I told him.

'Pillow grabbing is in, but leg grabbing is definitely out!' said Mr Watts.

We'd lost two Peg Men, and the pillow fight had only just started!

It got worse.

G. Dodd absolutely blasted my brother Leo in the next fight.

Ker-splosh!

Another Peg Man out!

The Big Road Eagles got three men into the semi-finals when Walter Bruce KER-SPLOSHED Wongy, although it didn't make much difference, because they were both in the Eagles.

The qualifiers for the semi-finals were H. Peg, R. Mitten, H. Abbott, G. Dodd and W. Bruce.

'Yah!' shouted Tom Small. '*Three* Eagles versus *two* Peg Men! Now we'll see who is the toughest.'

It was *three* against *one,* because Rosie Mitten wasn't a Peg Man, but we didn't tell him.

Shivery Lily Peg made the draw for the semi-finals.

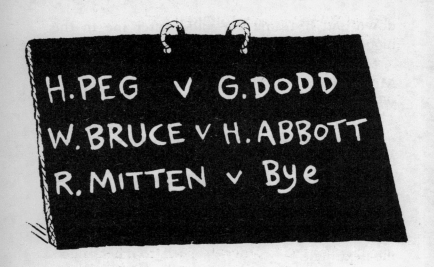

H.PEG v G.DODD
W.BRUCE v H.ABBOTT
R.MITTEN v Bye

It was another fix. We reckoned Lily had pulled a fast one because Rosie Mitten was a girl. First she got Piglet, who was small, and now she'd got a bye in the semi-finals.

'She'll go straight through to the final without fighting at all!' Hugh Abbott shouted.

'No she won't,' said Mr Watts. 'She'll fight a final eliminator against one of the other winners, and the winner of that will fight the other one in the final.'

'It will be all Eagles!' said Walter Bruce, flexing his muscles and trying to look like Superman.

'Oh no it won't!' said Henry Peg.

And WHAM! BAM! BOSH!
KER-SPLOSH!
Henry proved it.

G. Dodd was absolutely dumped into the water, and Henry Peg was the winner. All the Peg Men cheered like mad until our mums told us to shut up.

Mr Watts said he would stop the pillow fight if we kept making a racket. So we shut up and watched Walter Bruce ker-sploshing H. Abbott, which he did with one Monster Walter Blow.

Down went H. Abbott into the drink.

'Toss up for the final eliminator!' said Mr Watts, and Lily Peg had to unwrap herself from her mum's coat, put down her mug of beef tea and do the toss.

Henry Peg lost.

'I don't want to fight a soppy girl!' Henry said, going red.

'Yah! Scared!' said Walter Bruce.

Rosie Mitten didn't say a thing. She took off her glasses again, and put them on the towel. It was for drying her when she got knocked in the water, although she hadn't been knocked in yet. She got on the pole first this time, and worked her way out along it. She was good at it, for a girl.

Henry Peg got on, and they got their pillows.

'Do her with one blow, Henry!' Leo shouted.

'Yeah!' said Henry.

'Bash her in the drink!' I said.

'Ready?' said Mr Watts.

Henry nodded, and Rosie bent forward, as if she was saying something to Henry, although we couldn't hear it. Henry says it was 'Pudding Face' she said. It got him really mad.

'Steady!' said Mr Watts.

'Knock her block off, Henry!' Leo shouted.

'One blow!'

'GO!' shouted Mr Watts.

Rosie Mitten stuck her tongue out at Henry.

That made Henry even MADDER. He wanted to knock her head off with one big big blow, so he let fly.

Rosie Mitten ducked.

Henry missed.

When Rosie ducked, Henry's pillow went over her head, and Henry didn't let go. The pillow swung over Rosie Mitten, and away from the pole, and Henry started going after it, off balance.

Then
BIFF-BANG-SMASH-WALLOP.
Rosie Mitten let Henry have it. She hit him really hard, for a girl.
KER-SPLOSH!

Henry Peg went into the water, and all the Eagles cheered like mad. They started dancing and yelling and calling Henry Peg names because he had let a girl beat him.

We didn't say anything. We reckoned Rosie Mitten didn't fight fair, because she ducked.

'Hard luck, Henry,' I said to drippy Henry Peg as he climbed out.

'I'll fix her later!' Henry said. He was blue with cold, and cross. He wouldn't have lost if he hadn't been cold and slippy, and trying to knock her off with one blow.

Rosie Mitten sat there on the greasy pole, grinning at us.

'I bet Walter kills her!' Leo muttered.

Mr Bruce gave Walter his pillow, and they were all set for the Final Fight.

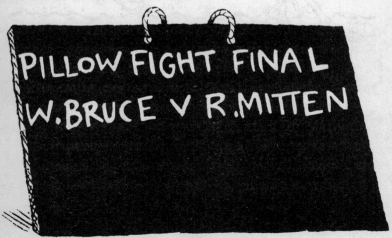

PILLOW FIGHT FINAL
W. BRUCE V R. MITTEN

'Ready?' Mr Watts said.

'The Eagles are going to win it!' I said. It was really naff!

'Steady?' said Mr Watts.

'Oh look!' said Rosie, pointing down. 'Jellyfish!'

Walter looked down at where she was pointing.

'GO!' shouted Mr Watts.

And . . .

BOFFFFFFFFF!

Rosie swung her pillow, and caught Walter right in his big belly, while he was still wondering where the jellyfish were.

Walter was wet and cold and greasy. Rosie's big pillow-bang started him slipping, and she followed up with BIFF-BANG-BIFF-BANG and . . .

KER-SPLOSH!

Walter was in the water, gasping.

The Big Road Eagles had stopped shouting. They stared down at Walter as though they couldn't believe their eyes.

'Araaah!' Walter said. 'Ugh!' His mouth was full of water.

Then Henry turned to me. *'We* won!' he said.

'Eh?' I said. 'But Rosie isn't . . .'

'Peg Men for ever!' shouted Leo, and then we all started shouting: 'We are the Peg Men!' until Mr Watts shut us up.

Rosie Mitten got her prize, which was a box of chocolates, and we all cheered her.

The Big Road Eagles looked green.

'She didn't beat me fair!' Walter Bruce muttered. 'It was a trick.'

'Buzz off, Walter. You can't take it. Just 'cause she's a girl,' Leo said.

I thought Walter was going to knock Leo's head off, but he didn't because Mr Watts was looking. He glared at Leo, and went off.

Henry Peg went up to Rosie.

'I ought to bash you,' he said.

'Don't be so stupid!' Rosie Mitten said.

She thought she was all right, because the grown-ups were still there, but they weren't. They'd all gone off to unfreeze Lily Peg in the Club House, Mr Watts included.

'Who are you calling stupid?' Henry said.

'You,' said Rosie.

'Right!' yelled Henry. 'That's it, then!' And he charged at Rosie Mitten to get his own back for being dumped in the drink.

I don't know exactly what Rosie did. She kind of grabbed his arm, and flipped him like a coin.

Henry went up in the air, and came down on his bottom.

'Anybody else?' Rosie said, blinking at us through her glasses.

Nobody moved.

'Bashing is stupid,' Rosie said.

'Stupid yourself!' Leo said, but he didn't go near her. I didn't say anything, but I stayed well out of her reach, just in case, and Piglet hid behind me.

We came off the land end of the harbour, well away from the club house, and that's where the Big Road Eagles were waiting for us, down by the fishing nets.

'Five, four, three, two, one . . . CHARGE!' Walter shouted.

We thought we were going to get scragged, but we didn't.

We didn't, because Rosie Mitten sort of stooped, just as the Eagles came dashing at us.

One minute she bent down, just as if she was tying her shoelace, and the next she pulled at the fishing net the Eagles were rushing across. It jerked, and tangled round their feet, and suddenly the Eagles were flying all over the shop and crash-landing on their ugly mugs.

'Grab the other end, Henry!' Rosie said.

Henry and Leo got one end, and Rosie and I and Piglet got the other. The Big Road Eagles were

caught in the middle. They were all tangled up.

'When I get out I'm going to bash you for sure, Rosie Mitten!' Walter shouted.

'Too bad!' said Rosie. 'All right, Henry. Tow them in the tar!'

There was tar all along the wall, where the men had been fixing the nets. We dragged the net towards it.

'We'll tell!' Tom Small yelled, desperately struggling to find his feet, and only getting tangled more.

'Oh yes?' said Rosie. 'Run home and tell your mum a *girl* caught you in a net, and towed you through the tar?'

'We're not telling that!' Walter Bruce said.

'Thought you wouldn't,' Rosie Mitten said. 'But *we* will. We'll tell every single person we meet how you got tarred. Unless you give up before you get tarred, of course.'

There was a long silence.

'All right!' Walter said.

'No bashing?' Rosie Mitten said, still keeping a tight hold on the net.

'No bashing,' Walter said.

'Let them go,' Rosie said.

We let go of the net, and the Big Road Eagles scrambled out. They cleared off, muttering threats about how they'd get us another time, and calling us names.

'You're dead tough, Rosie Mitten!' Piglet said.

'Yeah!' said Leo.

'You can be a Peg Man, if you want to,' said Henry Peg. 'We don't let soppy girls in the Peg Men, but you can be an honorary one.'

'No thanks,' said Rosie. 'I don't *like* bashing people, and I don't want to go round writing stupid things on walls.'

She went off.

'It's just as well she didn't join,' said Leo. 'She'd only get bashed. Then she'd cry, and run home to her mum, and there'd be trouble.'

'She *didn't* get bashed, though, did she?' I said.

'She didn't fight properly,' Henry Peg said.

'Girls never do!' Leo said.

'She just played tricks!' said Piglet scornfully, coming out from behind me, where he'd been hiding.

We walked up the lane.

'Just the same,' said Henry Peg. 'I reckon we should stay out of her way for a bit, don't you?'

And we do!

This story is by Martin Waddell.

Pale as Death

They came off the hills the next day soaked through to the skin. They not only had to take out all their outer clothes to the drying room but they had to change everything and have hot showers and an early bedtime. It had rained and rained and Mrs Boddington seemed to think they would all catch flu and die.

To make up for the early night, Mr and Mrs Boddington brought them hot cocoa in bed and told them all to snuggle up warmly.

'Mine's too hot,' whispered Caro. 'I'm going to save it.'

When Mr and Mrs Boddington had gone, they sneaked out of bed and gathered round the fire again, sipping their cocoa.

Colin looked round. 'Who's next?'

Janey jumped. 'Is it my turn?' she asked nervously.

'Have you got a story you would like to tell?' asked Colin politely.

'I don't know if I can tell you my story,' Janey whispered.

'Come on, Janey,' Caro said encouragingly. 'Don't be shy.'

'It's not that,' said Janey, looking at them with wide-open eyes. 'It's just that it frightens me to remember. I try not to think about it.'

'Did it really happen, then?' Even Damon had quietened down. Janey had a strange look on her face.

'Yes,' she admitted. 'You see, my story is true. You remember last term I had chicken-pox? Well, it's not supposed to be that serious these days, is it? Something went wrong with mine. I was really quite ill.'

'You did look ever so pale when you came back,' Caro nodded. 'My mum said so.'

'Yes. Pale. Very pale indeed.'

They stared at Janey, feeling uncomfortable. She seemed almost to be talking to herself.

'They sent me to stay with my aunt. She has a hill farm. Lots of fresh air but a long way from anywhere. No shops, no buses, no neighbours. And the house: so big, rambling and dark. Very dark.'

Janey pulled herself together and gave a little smile. 'I should start at the beginning. I was on the train all day. My mother came most of the way, but then we had to change. She put me on the local train and said my aunt would meet me at the other end. I had a list of stations to tick off. I waved to Mum and watched her run to get her train back. From that moment, I began to feel very lonely.

'It was getting dark. The train kept stopping but no-one seemed to get on or off. Then there was one more station, and we arrived at High Peak. I stepped down from the train and looked up and down the platform. There was no-one there. I even thought it was the wrong station and, in a panic, turned round to get back on the train. But it was already moving and the lights gradually disappeared, leaving the station darker than ever. Then I heard a voice, a whispering echo: "Janey". At the end of the platform was a tall, dark figure, perfectly still. "Janey," it said again, "I am your aunt."

'When I reached her, she spoke to me quite kindly. "You must be frozen, child. I am sorry to have kept you waiting. There were difficulties. Come, there is a good fire at home."

'She led the way outside and what do you think was there? Not a car. A pony and trap! I climbed

up and we drove out of the village and into the pitch-black country night.

'For a while there was just the sound of the pony's feet. Then the road began to climb steeply, and my aunt stopped the trap and got down.

'"You stay where you are, Janey," she said. "You have been ill," and she went to the pony's head and led it up the hill.

'Because she was a little way from me, I felt braver. "Is the farm in the mountains?" I asked.

'"Peak Farm," she answered. "It's in the pass, at the highest point."

'"It's so dark," I said. "How can you see?"

110

'"I cannot see," said my aunt. "The pony knows the way."

'Soon, I saw a point of light in the distance which gradually seemed to come nearer and nearer, until I realized it was a light in a window. It wasn't until we were nearly there that I saw that the dark behind the light was the shadow of a house. Not the low farm I was expecting, but a tall house, with turrets and many small windows. The door, however, was huge.

'It was strange,' said Janey, softly. 'My aunt had to turn the key with both hands, but then the door swung open easily, silently. We went into the kitchen which was warm, with a real fire blazing. Then my aunt lit a lamp on the scrubbed wooden table and I realized there was no electric light. Still, there was a pot of very good soup heating up on an old-fashioned range, and really delicious bread and cakes which my aunt baked herself.

'"No bakers up here, you see," she explained. "In fact, nobody calls at all. Come along now. I'll show you your room."

'She gave me a candle and took one herself. My bedroom was a high, dark room. There were shutters at the window and the bed was a four-poster with curtains round it. I really liked that, and the fact that I had my own old-fashioned bathroom leading off my room. It felt sort of royal. Like Balmoral, or something. My aunt checked the shutters.

'"Keep them closed, Janey," she said. "Always closed. Much more cosy like that."

'"What's this?" I asked, pointing to something on the bedside table. "Isn't that something you cook with?"

'"Garlic," said my aunt, after a moment's hesitation.

'"You *do* cook with it," I said, puzzled.

'"Yes," said my aunt. She paused again, then continued. "But rather pretty, don't you think? I keep it there to look at. Like a still life." She gave a short, dry laugh. "Yes, indeed. A still life."

'It seemed very strange to be in that high bed, the curtains partly drawn, but I was tired after my long journey. My aunt said goodnight and turned to go. At the door, she stopped.

'"If you should need me, my dear," she said, "call out to me. Do not hesitate. Call at once. Good night."

'I slept quite well. I was woken only once, by a tapping noise. I half sat up and looked towards the door, but then I realized the sound came from the shutters. "The wind must be blowing," I thought, and I was so tired I went back to sleep.'

Janey was quiet for a moment. She looked round at the still group. They all had their eyes fixed on her, almost as if they knew more than she did. They had moved closer together.

'Go on,' said Caro quietly.

Janey sighed.

'The next morning, the sun was shining and my aunt was singing in the kitchen. And that was what it was like all the time I was there. During the day, my aunt was wonderful. We went for walks and she told me the names of all the plants. I helped with the animals, and she also taught me how to cook. I got really good at it even though the range was so old-fashioned. But, as soon as the sun went down, I don't know . . . She sort of changed. She grew sad and quiet, and of course, I started those awful dreams. At least,' said Janey vaguely, 'I think they were dreams.'

Janey sank back in her chair. She seemed to have forgotten the others.

'Janey,' said Caro, softly, 'what did you dream about?'

'The first time,' continued Janey, 'I heard the tapping at the shutters again and I dreamed I went and opened them. A great bird was flapping at the window. I was frightened and slammed the shutters shut again. I jumped back into bed and started to shiver. The strange thing was, I wanted to open them and let the bird in. The second time, it was because I forgot to close the shutters before I went to bed.' She frowned. 'At least, I think I forgot. I became very muddled after the sun went down. Anyway, it must have been the full moon streaming in at the window that made me dream.

'The shadow of the great bird came to the window again. It seemed to speak: "Let me in. Let me in." I walked to the window in a daze and opened it. The shape slid in, like a silk scarf. It didn't look like a bird any more. More like a bat with fluttering wings. I couldn't really see. It moved between me and the door, but as it passed my bedside table, it whirled round, gave a horrid cry, then flew at me. I screamed and threw myself on the floor. I felt the air rush over my head as it escaped through the window, and the next moment, my aunt was there.

'She looked at the open window. "Janey, are you all right?"

'I told her what had happened. I noticed she glanced quickly at the bedside table.

'"There, my dear," she said, "what a nasty dream. I'll close the window and the shutters. Fasten them all nice and tightly. It's best to keep them shut, always."

114

'Strangely enough, the next day was especially nice. I was feeling much better. I would soon be out of quarantine and able to go home. I did all the cooking that day and made a really delicious dinner. I was quite proud of myself. But that was the night of the third and last dream.' Janey stopped and looked round. 'Sorry,' she said. 'I don't know why I'm telling you all this. I've been feeling so weak lately. Silly, really.'

Caro looked at her anxiously. 'Don't worry, Janey. Perhaps you were more ill than we realized. Perhaps you're not really over it.'

'What was the third dream like?' asked Midge.

Janey shuddered. 'I don't like thinking about it.'

They sat in complete silence. Outside, the wind began to rise, and rain began to flick against the window.

'Yes,' said Janey, dreamily, 'first there was a faint tapping at the glass, and then a more insistent knocking. The shutters were closed, of course, but I thought I heard a voice: "Come to the window. Come, Janey. Do not leave me outside."'

Janey seemed to be in a trance. They watched her, holding their breath. She suddenly moved her arm, jerking it towards the window. They all jumped. Janey continued her story in her little, low voice.

'I *had* to open it, you see. I found myself fumbling with the shutter bar, hurrying to undo the window latch. Then there was a great rush of air and it was there again, in the room. It was as if I suddenly woke up. It had seized my arm, rustling and flapping horribly. It seemed to be going for my throat. I screamed, and my aunt ran in through the door.

'"No! No!" she shouted. She ran to my bedside table but there was nothing there. "The garlic! For pity's sake! Where is it?"

'"I cooked it. It was in the stew."

'My aunt groaned and dropped to her knees and I knew nothing would stop the awful thing sinking its rotting teeth into me. I struck out but I felt a pain in my arm. And then, instead of attacking my throat as I had feared, it gave a ghastly gurgle and drew back. "Contaminated," it hissed. It was the only word it said, and it retreated through the window.

'My aunt rushed to fasten the shutters and then came to look after me. There were two holes in my arm. Two tiny holes.'

'"The fiend!" said my aunt in a low voice. "Saved by the chicken-pox, Janey," she added. Then she looked at me hard. "At least, I hope so."'

Janey glanced round at them. 'I don't know what

she meant exactly, but there were no more dreams and I came back home.'

No-one spoke.

'Poor old Janey,' Caro said at last, rather shakily.

'Very nasty,' said Damon, and they listened to the rain beating on the window.

'Of course, it was a dream,' said Caro.

'Yes, of *course* it was,' everyone agreed, but no-one was willing to make the first move to go to bed.

They all went in a bunch in the end, and very little was said in the girls' room, even though it took them a long time to get to sleep. The rain stopped, and gradually the clouds cleared and moonlight shone into the room.

Caro couldn't sleep at all. Something was niggling at the back of her mind. She remembered her mum saying that Janey had looked so pale, even after she had come back from her aunt's. Yes, that was it. Janey's mother had apparently said the poor girl wasn't much better for her holiday. She would have been better off at home.

'Janey!' Caro had suddenly remembered the rest of the conversation. She rolled over and looked at Janey in the bunk below her. In the moonlight, Janey looked up, her eyes wide open. 'Janey! Your aunt lives in Leicester! In a *flat*!'

Janey smiled and nodded. Then she brought a library book out from under her pillow and showed it to Caro. On the front was a tall, dark house. Bats fluttered round it.

'Janey!' hissed Caro, angrily. Then she started to giggle. The bunk bed rocked slightly as Janey started to laugh silently, too.

'Oh, Janey,' gasped Caro. 'You were winding us up! You were brilliant. We believed every word. Just you wait until tomorrow!'

This story is by Pat Thomson.

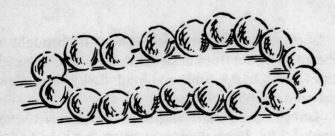

Pearls for the Giantess

In the old days there were giants about. There still are, of course, but fewer of them and they tend to be a great deal less trouble than they used to be. Nowadays there's none of this rampaging about the countryside tearing up trees, they leave that to the motorway builders. Neither do they go around terrifying little girls, most of whom would be more than a match for the average giant, who isn't very bright anyway.

In the old days, though, it was different. Giants rampaged and bullied all the time, rather like large sized toddlers – very large sized toddlers. If they didn't like something they stamped on it, and if they saw something they particularly fancied, well, they just took it. No questions asked.

There was one particular giant who took a fancy to Catriona.

Catriona was certainly a very fanciable young

lady. Small and plump with bright crisp ginger curls and a wicked twinkle in her eye. She was engaged to be married to Calum, the hunter and fisherman, and he, sensible lad, counted himself very lucky indeed. He was a good fisherman, but a bit soft-hearted for a hunter. He was more inclined to let the birds or animals escape, and even helped them to do so sometimes. There was one time he found a great golden eagle with a damaged claw, and spent weeks nursing it back to health.

'Daft!' said the local folk. 'It'll only come back and steal the lambs in the spring.' But that was Calum, a gentle big lad. Catriona loved him anyway, and he was devoted to her.

Not only was she pretty to look at, and a good cook, she could spin wool so fine people came from miles around to buy it. You can be sure they boasted about the quality of the clothes they made from Catriona's wool, and in time it came to the notice of a giant. He had never been one to bother about his clothes, but what others had, he must have too. He could not rest until he had a suit made from the finest wool. But giants do things their own way and instead of going along to Catriona's house, and putting in an order as everyone else did, he went along and removed Catriona. Lock, stock and spinning wheel.

Off he stamped to his castle, with Catriona kicking and screaming and threatening all sorts of trouble, but of course she never had a chance. He locked her up at the top of a high tower, along with her spinning wheel and a room full of rough fleece.

'No food for you until there's enough spun to make me a warm scarf to start with,' he roared. And that was that, she simply had to get on with it.

Calum of course was furious and threatened all sorts of revenge, but he had no idea where to start looking. The giant had come in the dead of night, and nobody had seen what way he went, but there was no stopping the lad.

'I'm a hunter,' he said. 'And I can surely track them down by myself.' He packed up his bow and arrows, locked up his cottage and tramped off into the hills.

He tramped for days, weeks and months through country that became bleaker and colder. He left behind the green straths with the little welcoming farmhouses and roamed high on the rocky shoulder of the mountains, but there was never a sign of the giant or Catriona.

He came at last to the top of a jagged peak and saw in every direction only more rocks, ice and bleak scree slopes. Calum sighed, slumped down, exhausted in the lee of the rocks and, with the whistling of the wind in his ears, fell asleep.

Some time later, he woke with a start, the wind had dropped because something stood in front of him, blocking the sunlight.

'Whit . . .?' He leaped to his feet, still dazed. Around his head the huge golden eagle wheeled and lifted and then gradually gliding down came to rest on the rock at his back.

'I had need of you once, brother,' said the eagle, 'but this day you have need of me, and I will repay my debt.'

'How? Tell me how?' Calum's head was spinning, as he watched the bird.

'I have seen the woman you seek,' it croaked. 'She lies imprisoned in a giant's tower many miles from here, high among mountains where no man has ever set foot. You have only to climb upon my back and I will take you to her.'

Calum needed no second invitation. Gulping back fear, he closed his eyes and threw his arms about the bird's neck. High above the mountains they soared, deep in the clouds where ice hung about them and his hands lost all feeling. Down they swooped into dark valleys where the pine trees grew tall and close in the sour earth and sun rarely shone. Then up again to a vast grey castle that seemed to grow like a shattered tree stump from the mountainside beneath it.

The eagle wheeled and circled. Far beneath them the heavy gates opened and a huge, shambling creature shuffled into the depths of the forests.

'He has gone hunting for the day,' said the bird. 'Now keep silence that his wife may not hear us, and we may leave safely with your lady.' With a stomach-churning swoop they swung down and landed on the window ledge of the highest room in the tower.

'Calum!' Catriona screeched, jumped back, and then threw her arms around him as he landed at her feet, frozen and terrified.

They clung together, speechless with delight. It would seem that all Calum's troubles were over, but not so.

'Hush!' he warned, but it was too late. A roar rattled the window panes. The stairs shook. A bolt shot back with a crash and the huge door was flung open. Standing before them, huge, stinking and ugly, was the giant's wife.

'You thocht to rescue the lassie did you?' she howled. 'We'll soon see aboot that, I'll have you in a stewpot for Himself in no time, young man.'

'Hang about a minute,' Calum protested as a huge hand reached out. 'Let's not be so hasty. You can't eat me before we've been introduced. The name is Calum.'

'Pleased to meet you I'm sure,' grunted the giantess, flashing him a horrible toothless smile. 'You'll be right nice in a pot wi' carrots and onions.'

'Just . . . just let me tell you a wee story,' said Calum dodging under a chair. 'You see, me and Catriona are very much in love.'

'Is that a fact?' She poked for him with a wooden spoon the size of an oar.

'Very much,' sighed Catriona, then she sniffed and started to cry.

'Och, for goodness sake stop it!' wheezed the

giantess, reaching for a filthy handkerchief the size of a tablecloth.

'And we're to be married,' said Calum. 'I've booked the church. My Grannie's made the cake and the most beautiful dress for Catriona.'

'Beautiful,' sniffed Catriona. 'All white, with pink roses.'

The giantess burst into tears and blew her nose so loudly the eagle was blown off his perch on the window-ledge. She was a romantic, kind-hearted soul, and deeply touched by the story.

'Tell you what,' she gulped in the end, 'as a special favour, I'll let you go . . .'

'Och thanks, Your Hugeness,' gasped Catriona and Calum.

'But on wan condition. You must get me the only thing I've always wanted. I've told Himself about if often enough, but does he listen? Not him . . .'

'I'll get it for you, whatever it is,' said Calum. 'Just tell me quick, before he gets back.'

'A necklace,' simpered the giantess. 'A great big pearl necklace. The sort of thing that will go with my best frock, and make me look really lovely. D'ye know whit ah mean?' She patted her greasy, grey hair and giggled horribly.

Calum nodded, stunned into silence. Where

would he ever find such a necklace?

'Bring me that and ye'll get yir wee lassie back, but not before. Do you hear me?' Calum was already hanging like grim death around the neck of the eagle and heading for home.

But there was no such necklace to be found, and even if there had been, where was he to find the money to buy it?

Calum was wandering along the beach late one evening pondering these problems, when there came a squeaking at his feet. He turned, and there were the otters playing in the pools left by the turning tide. Often enough before he had sat and watched them at their games and listened to their problems, now they listened to his.

'Pearls, is it?' squeaked the biggest otter. 'Ah well, you have to talk to the sea people for that. You've helped us often enough in the past, I don't see why we shouldn't help you now.' Before Calum had time to say another word, the otters were all about him, dragging him into the water.

Down and down they went, falling through the crystal green water, far deeper than Calum had ever swum before, but still the otters pulled him down until they came to the black mouth of an undersea cave. Through the tunnel he spun, twisting and turning, until he found himself pulled to his feet in a vast world of light and colour, where vaults of pink and white coral glowed in the green sea light, sparkling with precious stones.

The otters led Calum on to the innermost cave, and there in the Presence Chamber where the King of the Sea held court with his daughter, Calum told his story again.

The King listened with understanding, for Calum was known to him as a man of gentleness who had helped many sea creatures in the past.

'For a friend of our people I have pearls, and to spare. Go, fetch me such a necklace,' he ordered, and trusting only his daughter he gave her the key to his treasure cavern.

It would seem that Calum's troubles were over, but not so.

The Sea King's daughter was beautiful, but wilful. What she fancied she would have, and she fancied Calum. And so it was that she combed out her green hair, and returned with a necklace of pearls, each as large as a fist, and shining like the moon. In her other hand, though, she brought a deep shell filled to the brim with a wine known only to the fairy folk, a wine to delight the senses and steal the memory, the Elixir of Enchantment.

'Here are your pearls,' she said. 'But wait you now, the journey back is long and hard. Stay a

while, quench your thirst, and drink and eat with us.'

Calum drank, and with his thirst went the memories of his past life, his lost love, the giantess and her pearls.

So he would have lived happily enough, for ever and a day, had it not been for Catriona.

She sat spinning in the tower room, week after week, until the giant had scarves, tunics, pullovers and trousers enough to last him for ever, but still there was no sign of Calum. Gradually the giantess began to believe he would never come back and she allowed Catriona to come downstairs and sit with her in the hall.

One hot summer day Catriona begged to be allowed out of the castle to walk by the bank of the river at the foot of the mountain and there it was she met the salmon, and the two got chatting. She spun her wool, and he spun her a yarn or two concerning his travels around the oceans of the world. She told him the story of Calum and his quest for the pearls.

'But I fear he has forgotten me,' she sighed.

'I will find him for you,' said the salmon. 'But give me some token that I may remind him of you.' Catriona broke off a piece of the white wool she was spinning and tied it around the fish, who leapt flashing and spinning in the sunlight and vanished off down the river toward the sea.

In time he found the otters who remembered well how they had helped Calum. In time he found his way to the deep sea cave, through the dark tunnel and into the vaulted halls of coral. And not a moment too soon, for there was the Sea King, with all his court about him, preparing for the marriage of his daughter to Calum the fisherman.

A flick of his tail, a twist of his fin and the salmon circled Calum, flashing silver in the green light. But around him was tied the piece of white wool, a faint memory from the world that Calum had left behind. He reached out, and as his fingers untied the knot, the fairy spell was broken.

Back to his memory came Catriona, the giantess and the quest for the pearls which now hung about his own neck as wedding finery.

It was in vain that the Sea King's daughter wept, in vain that her father tried to plead. Calum must return to his own lost love. He threw his arms about the salmon and together they swept from the cave, up through the tumbling seas toward the land where the fresh water of the river mingled with the tides.

On and on they went, past the nets at the river mouth, skirting deep pools where men cast lines to catch the great fish, leaping waterfalls, on up the mountainside to the pool beneath the massive grey castle on the cliff.

Calum climbed from the water and hid in the bushes until he saw the giant lumber off to the hunting. Then quick as a flash he was through the gate before it swung shut, striding across the courtyard into the hall, where Catriona and the giantess sat on either side of the fire.

'A promise is a promise,' he declared. 'I have brought you the pearls.' He took the rope of huge beads from around his neck and threw it at the feet of the giantess who seized them joyfully.

'Awa' wi' ye. Quick noo, afore Himself gets

back,' she said, draping the pearls around her neck. She spat on her filthy handkerchief and tried to rub a clean spot on the mirror high above their heads.

'Lovely!' she said, arranging the beads beneath her chins. 'Pure dead brilliant!' And then a sudden thought struck her.

'Here, would you let me come to yir wedding in my best frock and . . .'

But Calum and Catriona never heard her. They were off down to the river and home.

This story is by Moira Miller.

A SELECTED LIST OF TITLES AVAILABLE FROM CORGI BOOKS

0 552 527688	**AMAZING ADVENTURE STORIES**	*Tony Bradman*	£2.99
0 552 52767X	**FANTASTIC SPACE STORIES**	*Tony Bradman*	£3.50
0 552 542962	**GOOD SPORTS: A BAG OF SPORTS STORIES**	*Tony Bradman*	£2.99
0 552 528374	**INCREDIBLY CREEPY STORIES**	*Tony Bradman*	£3.99
0 552 528153	**A BAND OF JOINING-IN STORIES**	*Pat Thomson*	£3.50
0 552 52817X	**A BARREL OF STORIES FOR 7 YEAR OLDS**	*Pat Thomson*	£3.99
0 552 527297	**A BASKET OF STORIES FOR 7 YEAR OLDS**	*Pat Thomson*	£3.50
0 552 527580	**A CHEST OF STORIES FOR 9 YEAR OLDS**	*Pat Thomson*	£3.99
0 552 528056	**A CRACKER FULL OF CHRISTMAS STORIES**	*Pat Thomson*	£3.99
0 552 527300	**A SACKFUL OF STORIES FOR 8 YEAR OLDS**	*Pat Thomson*	£3.50
0 552 527386	**A SATCHEL OF SCHOOL STORIES**	*Pat Thomson*	£3.99
0 552 52798X	**LONG TALES, SHORT TALES AND TALL TREES**	*Colin West*	£3.50